Tales of the Wild Horse Desert

NUMBER FOUR

Jack and Doris Smothers Series
in Texas History, Life, and Culture

TALES OF THE Wild Horse Desert

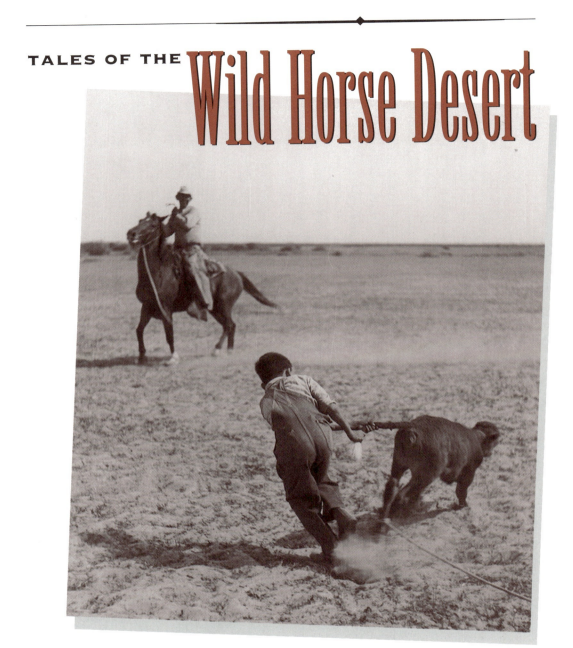

BETTY BAILEY COLLEY AND
JANE CLEMENTS MONDAY

UNIVERSITY OF TEXAS PRESS, AUSTIN

Publication of this work was made possible in part by support from the J. E. Smothers, Sr., Memorial Foundation and the National Endowment for the Humanities.

Title page photograph by Toni Frissell. Copyright © King Ranch, Inc., Kingsville, Texas.

COPYRIGHT © 2001 BY THE UNIVERSITY OF TEXAS PRESS

Printed in the United States of America

FIRST EDITION, 2001

Requests for permission to reproduce material from this work should be sent to Permissions, University of Texas Press, Box 7819, Austin, TX 78713-7819.

(∞) The paper used in this book meets the minimum requirements of ANSI/NISO Z39.48-1992 (R1997) (Permanence of Paper).

LIBRARY OF CONGRESS CATALOGING-IN-PUBLICATION DATA

Colley, Betty Bailey.
　Tales of the Wild Horse Desert / Betty Bailey Colley and Jane Clements Monday.
　　p.　　cm. — (Jack and Doris Smothers series in Texas history, life, and culture ; no. 4)
Includes bibliographical references (p.　) and index.
　ISBN 0-292-71241-3 (pbk. : alk. paper)
　1. Mexican American cowboys—Texas, South—Juvenile literature. 2. Mexican American families—Texas, South—Juvenile literature. 3. Ranch life—Texas, South—Juvenile literature. 4. King Ranch (Tex.)—Juvenile literature. 5. Kenedy Ranch (Tex.)—Juvenile literature. 6. Texas, South—Social life and customs—Juvenile literature. [1. Ranch life—Texas. 2. Cowboys. 3. Mexican Americans. 4. King Ranch (Tex.) 5. Kenedy Ranch (Tex.) 6. Texas.] I. Monday, Jane Clements, 1941– II. Title. III. Series.
　F395.M5 C65 2001
　976.4—dc21

2001000186

DESIGN AND TYPOGRAPHY BY TERESA W. WINGFIELD

CONTENTS

ACKNOWLEDGMENTS

Tales of the Wild Horse Desert for young readers is the book the authors had in mind when we first began interviewing the Kineños and Kenedeños. We were looking for Texas heroes and potential role models whose stories had not been told. The University of Texas Press chose to print the adult version first, and *Voices of the Wild Horse Desert* was published in 1997. We are grateful that the University of Texas Press is now making this book, based on the same interviews as the first, available for young readers. Our thanks go to Theresa May, Rachel Chance, Carolyn Wylie, Nancy Bryan, Brenda Jokisalo, and the rest of the Press staff.

Many people contributed to this book. We are grateful to Mr. Stephen "Tio" Kleberg of King Ranch and to Mr. James McCown and the John G. & Marie Stella Kenedy Foundation for their interest and cooperation. Thanks go also to Lorena M. García, secretary to the Kenedy Foundation, for her assistance.

We thank Mr. David Maldonado of King Ranch and Mr. Juan Guevara, formerly of the Kenedy Ranch, who served as valuable contacts to our interviewees.

To Mr. Bruce Cheeseman, former King Ranch Archivist, Lisa Neely, King Ranch Archivist, and Jamene Toelkes, Assistant Archivist, we express thanks for their expertise, assistance with research, and absolute dedication to accuracy.

We are grateful to our friend, Alberto "Beto" Maldonado, for his wealth of knowledge and warm support. We appreciate his entire family's help, especially that of his granddaughter, Sonia Maldonado García, who represented the new generation of vaquero family members so well.

Sincere thanks go to Dr. Billy Bowman, superintendent of Santa Gertrudis Independent School District. We appreciate Dr. Grace Everett, principal of Academy High School, Kingsville, and her staff for sharing with us the innovative programs available for students of vaquero families.

Thanks go to Dr. Donald Coers for providing invaluable technical assistance and support.

Cynthia Wright, social studies teacher in Pasadena Independent School District, provided invaluable support and suggestions on how the book can be used in the classroom.

To Charlie "Poppee" and Dorothy "Dee" Monday go thanks for providing our home away from home and for their continuous support of this project.

Sincere appreciation goes to our families for their interest and support. To our Monday children, Kimberly, Julie, Buddie, Jennifer, and Adam; and to our Colley children, Carey, Jill, and Steffen; and to Jessica Colley-Mitchell, who read the manuscript through the eyes of an eighth-grade student, go our sincere thanks. And to our husbands, Charles Monday and Burnham Jones, our most constant supporters, we can never express how much we appreciate their patience and unfailing belief in our work.

Finally, our deepest appreciation goes to our interviewees. They welcomed us into their homes, believed in our work, ignored the recorders and note pads, and spoke to us from their hearts. Our greatest hope is that we have accurately presented to young readers their stories of invaluable contributions to our heritage.

Nicolas

Nicolas lived in the Wild Horse Desert, a land of endless waving grass and searing heat in South Texas. He lived on King Ranch, one of several large ranches in this desert. Nicolas was born on the Ranch in 1898. His father died when he was six months old, and his mother worked hard to support her children.

Nicolas had held a paying job hauling water since he was eleven. The money he earned was spent for cloth, from which his mother sewed the family's clothing, and for shoes for his younger brother, Manuel, and sister, Marcela. With the five pesos his mother was paid as caretaker of the main entrance gate to the Ranch, plus the food rations furnished by the Ranch, the family was able to survive.

Then one day in 1915, everything changed. By now, Nicolas had a new job working in the fields. On this day, he went early to the fields as usual and worked all day, ending at dark. Near sunset he and his fellow workers heard popping noises that sounded like gunshots coming from the direction of El Hotel, the home of Caesar Kleberg, cousin to the owners of King Ranch.

Nicolas was afraid. The gunshots could mean that bandits were coming across the Rio Grande from Mexico again. Sometimes the bandits were Mexicans and sometimes they were Anglos, both looking to steal cattle from the big ranches. Some of the Mexican bandits were from families that had been former land owners in Texas, and they believed that

Texan lawyers, through unfair practices, had unlawfully taken their property. They sought revenge. There was a great deal of tension on both sides of the Rio Grande, the border between Mexico and Texas.

Nicolas's mother was working at El Hotel the day the shots were heard. She and all the other workers were terrified, and they quickly hid under the beds. As the bandits approached El Hotel, one of them put a rifle through the door and fired before entering.

When the gunshots ceased and all was quiet, Nicolas returned to El Hotel to find that his mother had been killed by a stray bullet. One story was that his brother Manuel lived only because a bullet hit his belt.

The bandits stayed until dark, kidnapping Manuel as they left.

These Texas Rangers, under the command of Captain Tom Tate, helped to defend the Norias Division of King Ranch against the bandit that killed Nicolas Rodríguez's mother. *Copyright © King Ranch, Inc., Kingsville, Texas.*

Manuel later told how he had been pulled up behind a bandit on horse-back as they fled. He managed to fall off the horse in the pitch-black night and hide in the grass. Then, after walking for hours, Manuel returned to El Hotel around two o'clock in the morning. He was finally joined there by Nicolas, who had hidden in a field when he heard the gunshots. The next day, Texas Rangers arrived by train to guard the Ranch, but their presence did not lessen the grief that Nicolas and his brother and sister felt.

Nicolas remembered his mother's funeral:

> Nobody came. It was only us, the children. It was dangerous at that time because of the bandits. Everyone was scared and, therefore, nobody came to the funeral for fear that the bandits would come back. There were like fifty rangers [Texas Rangers] in the hotel, and nobody could go out. It was 1915, and I was seventeen years old.

Nicolas Rodríguez became a vaquero, a Mexican cow-boy, on King Ranch. He is a descendant of this country's first cowboys. Vaqueros are the real cowboys on whose work the Anglo cowboy legend portrayed on movie and television screens is based.

> When the gunshots ceased and all was quiet, Nicolas returned to El Hotel …

Vaqueros are descendants of the Spanish settlers and Mestizos, people with a blend of Spanish and Indian blood. Their origins stem from experienced horse-men who came from Spain to Mexico in the 1500s and passed their expertise on to the native Indians. The vaqueros worked on the grand haciendas (large ranches) of northern Mexico and later came to the Wild Horse Desert in Texas to share their knowledge of cattle and horses. Some of these vaquero families have worked on the King and Kenedy Ranches for more than one hundred years.

These vaqueros and their families have many stories to tell of their highly skilled work with some of the most prized cattle and horses in the world. Their tales recount their important contributions to America's cattle industry and to the settling of the Southwest.

CHAPTER ONE

The True Cowboys

The *entrada* (procession) of men, women, children, goats, chickens, cattle, dogs, pack-saddled burros, and horses pulling *carretas* (carts) with the villagers' possessions piled high must have been quite a sight. Moving slowly across flowing waves of tall grass stretching as far as they could see, the more than 120 citizens were leaving their home in Cruillas, Mexico, for a new home on the Wild Horse Desert in South Texas. While Indians occasionally came into the region to hunt and capture horses, the land the *entrada* traveled was a stretch of mostly uninhabited land except for wild mustangs, Longhorn cattle, and a few brave settlers. A young steamboat captain named Richard King had come to their village seeking to buy livestock and find laborers who knew about cattle ranching. He persuaded most of the people of Cruillas to bring all their belongings and make their home at his new cow camp.

The year was 1853, and Captain King was beginning a bold new venture with this ranch. Captain King's steamboating partner, Captain Mifflin Kenedy, later became a partner in the ranch. After a few years, Kenedy developed his own ranch next to King's, and the two

VAQUEROS COME TO SOUTH TEXAS

- during Spanish rule prior to 1821

- during Mexican rule (1821–1836)

- following the American Civil War (1861–1865)

- during the Mexican Revolution (1910–1920)

Captains Richard King (left) and Mifflin Kenedy were friends and business partners. They established the King and Kenedy Ranches in the Wild Horse Desert and were leaders in the founding of the American cattle industry. *Copyright © King Ranch, Inc., Kingsville, Texas.*

Xavier Quintanilla, Valentín Quintanilla's father, with his wife, Teresa. The Quintanilla family probably came to the Ranch from the Mexican village with Captain King. They have worked with the King Family for over 140 years.

ranches operated as neighbors. Though these ranches developed their own unique characteristics, King and Kenedy borrowed heavily from the tradition of the great Mexican ranches.

To the south in northern Mexico, great haciendas (large rural estates) provided Mexico with beef, hides, and tallow (fat). Some of the larger spreads contained from 500,000 to more than a million acres and were thriving enterprises. Several of the Mexican vaquero families from these ranches had ventured into the Wild Horse Desert and started cattle operations of their own. King found some of them there as he traveled on horseback from Brownsville to the port city of Corpus Christi in the early 1850s. It was during this trip that he had the idea to establish a cattle and ranching business on the Wild Horse Desert. He chose a site on Santa Gertrudis Creek near Corpus Christi for his first purchase.

Captain King had earned the money for his ranch by running steamboats on the Rio Grande during the Mexican-American War (1846–1848). However, he had a problem. He knew a lot about steamboating, but he knew nothing about cattle ranching. As soon as he had bought his land, King sensed that he faced a huge challenge. He realized that he must have expert knowledge to turn this vast desert into his dream of a profitable cattle and ranching enterprise. From visits with friends in Brownsville and hacienda owners along the Rio Grande, King had heard of the expertise of the vaqueros in Northern Mexico, and he turned to them for help.

The people who were traveling with King from Cruillas to Santa Gertrudis had all the skills Captain King needed. Their Spanish ancestors had developed horseback handling of cattle on the open range. This knowledge was handed down from one generation to the next. The Cruillas vaqueros were skilled at throwing a rope of rawhide they had made themselves. They were skilled at throwing a sliding noose from the back of a horse while riding on a saddle they had invented for this work. They knew just how to train horses for the jobs of herding and roping cattle. King also employed some of the vaquero families that were already living in the Wild Horse Desert. All of this knowledge would be necessary for Richard King and his friend Mifflin Kenedy in the development of their

IMPORTANT DATES

- Texas Statehood, 1845

- Mexican-American War, 1846–1848

- Rancho Santa Gertrudis (Later King Ranch), 1853

- Kenedy Ranch (Los Laureles), 1868

- Kenedy Ranch (La Parra), 1882

- World War I, 1914–1918

- World War II, 1941–1945

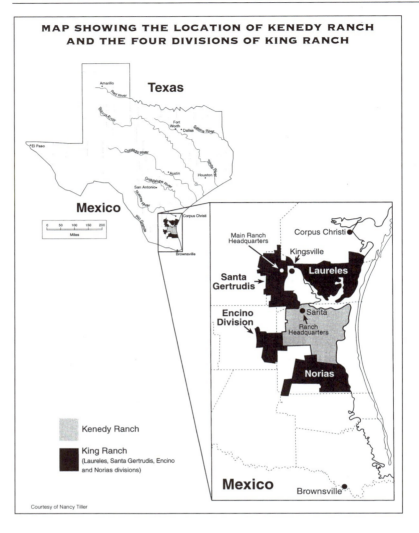

MAP SHOWING THE LOCATION OF KENEDY RANCH AND THE FOUR DIVISIONS OF KING RANCH

Courtesy of Nancy Tiller

The early inhabitants of the Wild Horse Desert lived in *jacales* (straw, mud, and wood houses) in the late 1800s.

Copyright © King Ranch, Inc., Kingsville, Texas.

Ramón Alvarado was one of the first vaqueros on King Ranch. He helped his father build the first *jacales* (houses made of straw, mud, and wood) on the Ranch in 1854. He served as Captain King's bodyguard and was a "cow boss" in the 1880s.

ranches. The vaqueros were this country's first true cowboys. They enabled the King and Kenedy Ranches to make vital contributions to the development of this country's cattle industry, which would help to feed the nation.

When the vaqueros arrived at Santa Gertrudis in 1853, they started from almost nothing in this wild land. They were faced with building housing and ranch structures, taming horses, corralling and taking care of cattle, and maintaining water holes. In this isolated land, there were no towns for shopping, hospitals for the sick, nor law enforcement in times of trouble. Of necessity, the vaqueros and the ranch owners had to rely on each other. On King Ranch, and later on Kenedy Ranch, a very special relationship between the vaquero families and the owners developed from mutual need. Each depended on and respected the other. Together these families faced hardships and dangers—rough, unforgiving terrain, storms, drought, blistering sun, rattlesnakes, feral (wild) hogs, wars, and Indian and bandit raids. Their lives became intertwined as they shared work, celebrations such as weddings and births, and grief at times of sickness and death. Olga Serna on Kenedy Ranch explained:

> The families are very close—they support each other. When one hurts, all hurt. In Kenedy Ranch we have friendship, security, and unity.

Both owner and vaquero families lived with danger. Nicolas Rodríguez told a story about Indians kidnapping his great-aunt around the turn of the century (1900):

Olga Serna, a third-generation vaquero family member, and her husband, Enemorio Serna, a second-generation vaquero, brought up their family on Kenedy Ranch in Sarita, Texas.

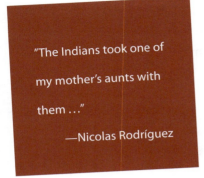

"The Indians took one of my mother's aunts with them ..."

—Nicolas Rodríguez

The Indians took one of my mother's aunts with them. She was pregnant, and she lived in a small house. The Indians were both women and men and they were all riding horses. The Indians also had with them a young man who spoke Spanish. They had raised him, and he took care of their horses. One day, the Indians left the boy in charge of my aunt and they [the Indians] all left. The young man took two of the best horses, and told my aunt that they were going to escape. They both went all the way to the Rio Grande—I am not sure how far away that was—and crossed the river. They crossed the river on horses. The Indians were all on the other side and could not do anything about their escape. The Indians almost caught them because my aunt and the young man had just crossed the river when the Indians showed up on the Texas side of it.

Compared to many cowboys, these vaqueros had a better way of life. As a way of saving money, most Western (Anglo) ranch owners hired workers only during the busy times such as roundups in the spring and fall. During the winter months they were left to fend for themselves, and they often drifted from place to place, managing as best they could. Stable employment necessary for settling down and establishing families was rare. In contrast, the vaqueros on the King and Kenedy Ranches became permanent workers. On King Ranch, they and their families lived year round. Kenedy hired skilled vaqueros from nearby ranches in the Rio Grande area on a continuing basis, and they became permanent employees and residents of Kenedy Ranch. These vaqueros and other workers on the ranches became known as Kineños (King's Men) and Kenedeños (Kenedy's Men) because of their important role on these ranches. Some of the vaquero families stayed on the ranches for four and five generations. The Kineños and Kenedeños were quiet, hard-working, law-abiding folk with courage, skill, and genuine pride in their work. They became the stable work force that made a significant difference in the success of both ranches.

Life was not always easy for either owners or workers, and harmony did not always exist. But their lives were bound by common threads of respect and loyalty. They knew that the well-being of both depended on their working together. Kineños were sometimes caught in the midst of political battles and wars that involved the owners. This dilemma is perhaps best illustrated by a story about Francisco Alvarado and the King family during the American Civil War (1861–1865).

Captain King was a Confederate, and he was afraid that some day the Yankees (Union troops) might come to the Ranch and harm him or his family because he was considered the enemy. His fears were realized one day when he was away from the Ranch. Because Francisco Alvarado was one of the most trusted servants, Captain King had chosen him to stay in the house and protect his family in his absence. Mrs. King told Francisco of the possible danger and urged him to notify her if he noticed anything unusual. Francisco was sleeping on a cot in the hall where noises could be more easily heard when, sure enough, a troop of Yankees entered the yard and began shooting guns at the house. Francisco moved quickly to tell them not to shoot their guns because Captain King was away and only the family was there. Before he could speak, the soldiers fired at his shadow, and Francisco fell dead on the porch. There were some Mexicans in the troop of Yankees who were friends of the Alvarado family, and they were sorry for shooting Francisco by mistake.

> Before he could speak, the soldiers fired at his shadow, and Francisco fell dead on the porch.

Three generations of Silvas on King Ranch. *Photograph by Toni Frissell. Copyright © King Ranch, Inc., Kingsville, Texas.*

The special roles of the Kineños and Kenedeños extended beyond their abilities with livestock. The early Kineños also served as guards for Captains King and Kenedy during the days when they traveled on the road between the Ranch, Corpus Christi, and Brownsville. King often took four or five armed vaqueros with him. Stagecoach camps were set up about every twenty miles with fast horses ready in case there was trouble from bandits, because King carried a payroll that could amount to as much as $50,000. When King was away from the Ranch, he depended on vaqueros to carry the payroll.

Besides guarding the payroll, Kineños furnished other protection. In 1875, Kineños were called on to protect King Ranch from Mexican bandits. When the bandits surrounded the Ranch Headquarters, the Kineños successfully turned them back.

On Kenedy Ranch, José María Morales, who was a *mayordomo* (boss) of supply wagons and a caporal (cow boss), also traveled the dangerous roads between La Parra, Kenedy Ranch Headquarters, and San Antonio. Though he was followed and had some close calls with would-be robbers, José, heavily armed, always arrived with the payroll.

Vaqueros also took good care of owner families when they traveled. During the 1870s, King family members made many trips to San Antonio. King's daughter, Alice, remembered the campfires by the road at night and the guard of armed Kineños. She told of the rumble of the moving wheels of the King Ranch wagon train, paced by outriders sweeping through high grass on fast horses with manes and tails flowing.

The vaqueros developed a fierce, independent spirit full of pride and accomplishment. They approached their tasks with dedication and a sense of duty. Faustino Villa was a vaquero who had been with King since the days when he worked as a deckhand while King was running his steamboat, the *Colonel Cross*, on the Rio Grande. Villa refused to accept retirement from the Ranch. He explained, "When Faustino Villa gets so he can't earn grub, he'll be ready to go." He got his wish and remained on the payroll, riding horseback until two weeks before his death. One of his jobs was delivering the mail. At one hundred years of age, Faustino swam a half-mile across the flooded Santa Gertrudis Creek to deliver the mail to *el abogado* (the lawyer), Robert Kleberg, King's son-in-law, who was in charge of King Ranch after Captain King's death.

Another story was told of Ignacio Alvarado, who displayed the same dedication to his work. Ignacio, who was the caporal, was late to take charge of a herd and move it. Two days went by. Finally, Ignacio's son appeared and said, "My father says to tell you he was sorry he could not come. He had to die."

Appreciation of the contributions of the "original cowboys" was well said in 1997 by Stephen J. "Tio" Kleberg, then vice president of King Ranch, Inc., and family member resident manager of King Ranch, now a member of the Board of Directors. In his foreword to a book, *Voices of the Wild Horse Desert*, he wrote:

> *Los Kineños* are my extended family. Having lived and worked almost my entire life on King Ranch, I am firmly convinced that the people and culture of this ongoing enterprise are its greatest asset. To them, and to the Mexican American culture which created the character and success of King Ranch, I conclude by repeating the dedication offered in Tom Lea's magisterial history, *The King Ranch*, published in 1957:
>
> > A todos aquellos hombres [To all those men]
> > Kineños de verdad [the true Kineños]
> > Se dedica esta obra [this work is dedicated]
> > En reconocimiento de lo que [in recognition of what]
> > Les debe este rancho [this ranch owes them].

Thus, a special relationship of loyalty, dependability, and mutual respect has been a binding factor between owners and workers on the King and Kenedy Ranches since the very beginning, almost six generations ago.

CHAPTER TWO

Growing Up on the Wild Horse Desert

"Levántate" ("Time to get up"), his mother said gently. It was 5:00 A.M., and time for the boy's day to begin. Alberto "Beto" Maldonado put his feet on the hard plank floor and dragged himself out of a deep sleep caused by a combination of fresh air and a fourteen-hour work day. Pulling on the clothes he wore yesterday, he trotted twenty-five yards to the outside toilet. Next, he quickly walked the quarter-mile to the barn with his father and brothers to his first "boy job" of the morning, milking the family cow and feeding the calves. His father, Librado Maldonado, was in charge of the dairy operation of the famous Jersey herd, so Beto's boy jobs began in the dairy barn. With the cows milked, Beto then worked at his job of teaching calves, soon to be weaned from their mothers, how to drink milk from a bucket. This was a tricky task, even for an adult. Coaxing the calf to the bucket, Beto stuck his fingers in the bucket of warm milk. He rubbed his hand across the soft, velvety lips of the baby calf, moved it to the nostrils to let the calf smell, then back to its lips, enticing the calf to suck the milk from his fingers. Again and again, Beto and the calf practiced until the calf finally learned to drink directly from the bucket. Beto knew from his father that this was a very important step in getting the calf to put on weight at the fastest possible rate. Every morning Beto and his brother, Lee (Librado Jr.), worked with their calves, moving them from mother to bucket. The five dollars a month they earned for this work was big money.

Alberto "Beto" and Librado "Lee" Maldonado prepare their calves for competition. *Courtesy of Alberto "Beto" Maldonado.*

Alberto "Beto" Maldonado (left) and his brother, Librado "Lee" Jr., show their King Ranch Santa Gertrudis bull calves at the County Fair in 1940. Beto's calf won a blue ribbon, and Lee's calf placed second, the first wins for the Santa Gertrudis breed developed on King Ranch as the first American cattle breed.
Courtesy King Ranch Archives, King Ranch, Inc., Kingsville, Texas.

And there were other rewards. One of the proudest days of Beto's life was when he and Lee brought their Santa Gertrudis calves to compete in the Kleberg County Fair. Under the careful, expert eye of their father, they had tended the calves from the very beginning, and this would be the day for all the world to see the results of their hard work—Beto's calf would win a blue ribbon, and Lee's would place second. Many years later, Beto's eyes twinkled as he described what happened next: "One calf won first place, and I believe this was the first win for the new Santa Gertrudis breed. I was so proud of that blue ribbon that I took it home and put it in the stall in the barn and was disappointed to find when I turned around that the calf had liked it, too, and had eaten it."

The dairy operation was serious business to their father, and roping one of "his" famed King Ranch Jersey herd was strictly forbidden. But sometimes Beto and Lee could not resist roping these calves. Calves were the perfect target for the boys' lasso practice with their new ropes, but if they got caught, they would be in big trouble with their father.

By 6:30 A.M., Beto was back home to change into his clean, hand-sewn pants and shirt, which were usually white or khaki-colored. He carefully removed them from his clothes box. He had two sets of clothes, and today his mother would wash the set he wore yesterday, press them with the iron heated on the wood-burning stove, and place these clean clothes in his box for him to wear tomorrow. He scrubbed his hands up to his elbows, washed his face, and neatly combed his straight black hair. Finally dressed, he ate his breakfast of eggs, potatoes, and fresh flour tortillas his mother made. He picked up his lunch of fried steak wrapped in tortillas and reached for the reader he had struggled with last night. He had secretly hoped for a store-

Young boys on King Ranch riding their horse, perhaps to school. *Photograph by Toni Frissell. Copyright © King Ranch, Inc., Kingsville, Texas.*

bought lunch from the Ranch's store, called the Commissary, of potted meat (3¢) and crackers (5¢), but this rare treat cost money and would have to wait until a special occasion. Today, he would eat the lunch his mother had prepared. He could expect no candy or fruit, but unlike those of most of the other children, Beto's lunch did include a special treat. His mother was very good at baking yeast-based sweet rolls and breads in the wood stove, a rare talent among the ranch women, and so he would be the envy of his friends when they smelled the spicy cinnamon rolls he brought today. His drink, as usual, would be water from the faucet at school.

A boy rings the school bell on the Norias Division of King Ranch.

Photograph by Toni Frissell. Copyright ©King Ranch, Inc., Kingsville, Texas.

He set off for the mile walk. Later he would have a Shetland pony to ride to school, but today he walked. Some of his luckier classmates would arrive on horseback because they lived four miles away.

At the ranch-owned Santa Gertrudis School, which Beto attended in the late 1930s, classes lasted from 8:00 A.M. to 3:00 P.M., with a recess (play period) in the morning and another in the afternoon. After he gobbled down his lunch, Beto and his friends raced off to play baseball or marbles during the hour allotted for lunch. On chilly days, part of their lunch hour would be spent splitting the wood for the school's wood-burning stove and hauling it in a wheelbarrow.

Beto had spoken Spanish all his life. All of the Kineño families and owners spoke Spanish, and the Ranch owners saw to it that their children learned Spanish before they were old enough to go to school. Spanish was the language of the Ranch. For some reason which Beto could not figure out, Spanish was outlawed at school. It was neither taught nor spoken. Beto felt scared and frustrated because he could not understand what the teacher was saying.

"I was not fluent in English when I started," Beto explained, a pained expression returning to his face as he remembered. "It was very diffi-

Santa Gertrudis School, 1926. From the José Arredondo Collection. *Copyright © King Ranch, Inc., Kingsville, Texas.*

Students in the school located on the Santa Gertrudis Division of King Ranch in 1946. Top Row: José E. Mendietta, Jesús Rodríguez, Israel Mendietta, Rubén Flores, Arnold Mendietta, Domingo Salinas, Hector Arredondo. Middle Row: Gilberto García, Juan Salinas, Gloria Cavazos, Eleberto Quintanilla, Ricardo Gonzales, Englantina García, María Salinas, Mrs. Ellis, Magdalena Treviño, Carlos Escobedo, María Luisa Silguero, Julián Buentello Jr., Raquel Rodríguez, Emerardo Quintanilla. Bottom Row: Edna Sáenz, Armando Mendietta, Ramona Ricón, Victoriano García, Guadalupe Rodríguez, Celestino Quintanilla Jr., Olga Silguero, Robert Lower, Josefa Mendietta, Victor Cavazos, Gloria Rosas, Hipolito Silguero. *Photo by Pollo Filguero. From the Pollo Filguero Collection, courtesy King Ranch Archives, King Ranch, Inc., Kingsville, Texas.*

cult." Beto and his friends whispered Spanish to each other at lunch and recess so they wouldn't get in trouble for speaking their forbidden language.

Beto entered the wood-framed school and cautiously went into one of the two classrooms. One classroom held grades 1 through 4, and the other held grades 5 through 8. The two rooms could be opened up to make one big room where dances were held. Each classroom had one teacher. Beto labored over the strange-sounding English words. Next, he and his classmates studied mathematics (arithmetic). Beto took his turn at the blackboard, adding and subtracting sets of numbers with chalk and eraser in hand. After that, he wrote spelling words in his "Big Chief" tablet. By fifth grade, Beto would study maps of the world in geography class, and this excited him. But he could not have dreamed that, one day, he would travel to one of those strange-sounding places—to Morocco—on an airplane with show cattle of the world-famous King Ranch. His father was the top cattle showman for the Ranch. He would help his father, Librado, introduce the first American cattle breed—the Santa Gertrudis— to the King of Morocco and to the African continent.

After school, Beto usually could not resist a quick game of marbles, but on this day he played hurriedly. There would be much work waiting for him back at home.

After walking home, Beto chopped wood and carefully stacked it on the pile so it would be ready for fires in the cook stove, which doubled as a heater in winter. Next he went to the dairy barn and began raking stalls and preparing feed. He worked there with his father until 6:00 or 7:00 at night. He never wondered why the job was necessary, and there

Librado Maldonado and his son, Alberto "Beto," flew to Morocco with the Santa Gertrudis cattle to introduce them to the African continent.
Courtesy of Alberto "Beto" Maldonado.

Ella Maldonado with twin daughters Amelia and Aurora. The Maldonado family has been on King Ranch for four generations.

was no discussion as to whether he would do it. It was expected, and, like the other Kineño children, he did what he was told.

The family then gathered for their evening meal. Fresh tortillas, beans, and sometimes rice made up the menu. There was always plenty of whole milk with cream on top so thick it needed to be stirred before drinking. There was no such thing as a grocery store with homogenized milk on the Ranch.

After supper, Beto's boy jobs continued. He tended the calves, brought in wood for the stove, and did any other job assigned by his father and mother. Next his mother and older brothers would try to help him a little with his English, and he could be in bed by 9:00 or 10:00. But not before his nightly bath. Beto filled the big no. 3 metal tub with water from the faucet outside. The water would feel cool and refreshing after the long, hot, dusty day. Washing with soap his mother had made of lye (liquid made by filtering water through wood ashes) and tallow, Beto removed the dirt he had picked up from his long day on the Wild Horse Desert. As for every other child of Kineño families, this was a nightly ritual, every night, hot or cold, summer or winter. At this warm time of year Beto was just glad the water needed no heating, because, if it did, after his bath he would have to build a fire under another tub so that hot water would be available for the rest of his family. Tonight he could just slip into his bed.

Boys began learning ranching skills by doing "boy jobs" at around age seven. *Photograph by Toni Frissell. Copyright ©King Ranch, Inc., Kingsville, Texas.*

*   *   *

Two generations ago, Kineño and Kenedeño sons and daughters knew they would grow up to work on the Ranches, and they could learn what they needed to know from their parents. School, especially English, had little meaning for them. The few children on King Ranch who finished eighth grade attended high school in Kingsville, the nearest town. If they went at all, students on Kenedy Ranch attended high school in the nearby towns of Riviera or Raymondville. Most of the students from both ranches dropped out of school by the time they were thirteen or fourteen, and Beto was no exception. After one year in town, Beto dropped out. He missed school more than he thought he would and often dreamed of being back there. When GED (General Education Diploma) classes began, he finally went back to school when he was fifty years old and completed his GED. He and his family—especially his mother—were so proud that they had a big family party and Beto got gifts. He even wore his daughter's cap and gown for the celebration.

Alberto "Beto" Maldonado borrowed his daughter's graduation robe for his party to celebrate earning his General Education Degree (GED) at age fifty.

*   *   *

Like Beto and Lee, all boys began learning their life's work doing "boy jobs." They soon learned that jobs on the King and Kenedy Ranches fell into two categories: those worked from horseback and those worked on foot. Rounding up and branding cattle were the main tasks of the vaqueros on horseback. Getting rid of ticks and vaccinating livestock against disease was also part of their job. The workers on foot did dozens of other jobs necessary to the operation of the Ranches. Some of these jobs included working with the veterinarian in the cattle and horse breeding programs, tending windmills so the families and animals would have water, and building and mending fences—2,000 miles of them on King Ranch alone. Workers on foot also helped cut brush, build buildings, cook, drive trucks, and help the owners with hunts and entertainment of guests. The fathers taught the boys that it was important to learn as many skills as possible so they would always have a job.

Though Kineño and Kenedeño chil-

The dipping vat was invented on King Ranch in 1891 to rid cattle of ticks that caused Texas tick fever. Vaqueros moved the cattle through the vat filled with a solution of medicine that killed the ticks. Today, cattle are sprayed to kill ticks.

dren had many chores that were necessary for the family, they sometimes had a little time to play. Young boys' favorite toy was a stick horse made from a straight stick found in the pasture or from an old broomstick. Girls played with dolls they made of cornhusks. Toys were scarce, but imaginations were not. Stella Guevara on Kenedy Ranch said that she and her young

Juan Guevara Jr., a fourth-generation vaquero when he worked on Kenedy Ranch, told of playing vaqueros as a child.

friends used a sharp stick to "make a house" by drawing an outline in the pasture dirt. They drew the same rooms that were in their real houses, usually a kitchen and two bedrooms. They made tortillas of mud and water and tamales of large leaves wrapped around mud. They served their "food" on "plates" of Mason jar lids. The boys often played with the girls, riding off like vaqueros on their stick horses. Stella's son, Juan Guevara Jr., played the same way. Stella's mother, Teresa Mayorga Cuellar (born in 1915) told Stella she and her friends played the same way, except that the boys actually killed small animals, built fires, and cooked their meat.

Kineño and Kenedeño children often played with children of the owners and bosses. Though both groups were aware of their different backgrounds, it did not affect the many hours they spent together as friends. Spanish was their common language. Manuel Silva (born in 1905) remembered playing with Richard Lee King. "I learned to shoot when I was twelve. I was always with Don Ricardo. When I got home from school I used to go into the stables with him, and he would shoot pennies that I threw in the air." María Luisa Montalvo Silva grew up on King Ranch. She said, "I was friends with Mary Burwell. Her father was the caporal of Laureles. My Grandpa, Pedro Montalvo, taught us both to ride. We would ride every afternoon after school. He would have the horses ready and he would ride with us." It may have been during these rides that María Luisa decided that, one day, she would become one of the few women ever to work as a vaquera on King Ranch.

Boys began formal training for their life's work at age seven or eight when they were assigned boy jobs. They learned practically everything they knew by tagging after and imitating their fathers. Plácido L. Maldonado grew up on King Ranch during the 1920s and 1930s. He said,

"I first remember being with Dad at ten. I went to the barn with him and would sweep and do other jobs. My first payroll job was at thirteen or fourteen. I raised calves."

Common boy jobs were chopping wood, milking cows, feeding animals, cutting grass, working with the tamed oxen, or helping the cook. During this time, young boys also learned to respect adults. Miguel Muñiz of King Ranch said, "I carried water for a boy job. I would fold my arms while waiting for the men to drink to show respect. Then I would take the cup back. I would kiss my mother's and father's hands to show respect. I always took off my hat to show respect."

When they were not doing boy jobs, Kineño and Kenedeño sons practiced roping. First they learned to tie a knot, then pull the rope through the small opening to make a loop. They began by using a big loop to rope fence posts because the posts wouldn't move. After hours and hours of practice, the boys were ready for moving targets, and chickens, pigs, turkeys, rabbits, and dogs were no longer safe. The goal was to use the small-

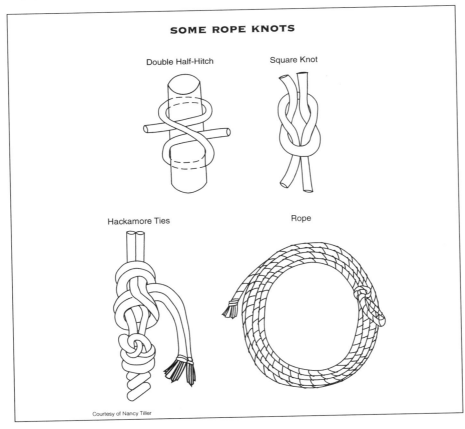

SOME ROPE KNOTS

Double Half-Hitch

Square Knot

Hackamore Ties

Rope

Courtesy of Nancy Tiller

A future vaquero learning his "boy job" of catching young calves on the range at King Ranch. *Photograph by Toni Frissell. Copyright © King Ranch, Inc., Kingsville, Texas.*

est loop possible to just go over the neck of the target. This skill would be necessary later on for holding a calf for branding.

Once the boys had some skill at roping, they began learning to ride. Enemorio Serna learned by riding calves. Every day he would watch the vaqueros ride the sleek, shiny Quarter Horses, and he longed for the day when he, too, would ride the finest. He had to start somewhere, and riding calves, though forbidden, was his only chance. By age seven he knew how to lasso a calf and pull it to the fence, where he could climb on. He would hang on as long as possible. Of course, the calf did not plan to have a boy on its back. The game was to see how long Enemorio could stay on. Riding bareback without a bridle was not easy. Time after time he climbed back on until, finally, he could ride the calf. He could hardly wait until he was older and could practice riding on a pony.

After the son had mastered boy jobs and had at least some skill in riding and roping, he would begin going out to the cow camps with his dad. This was usually at age twelve to fifteen. At first he rode in a wagon, watching, learning, waiting to prove himself, and then grabbing the first opportunity to graduate to a horse. Only then could he begin learning what he really needed to know. Now he could begin his cow camp work by learning how to lasso and throw a calf for branding. He also learned to separate or "cut" cattle from the herd. One of the expert vaquero ropers would teach him. Martín Mendietta Jr. of King Ranch said, "You gave the horse who knew the most to the young kid so he could learn from the horse. He just had to stay on, and the horse would move the animal."

Next, the boys on the Kenedy and King Ranches were trained to round up cattle from the brush, cut them for branding or penning, and rope and tie three legs of a calf so it could be branded. One of their hardest lessons was learning to round up and break horses. Later, some of the Kineños would learn to show to the rest of the world the prize cattle and horses that symbolized King Ranch. Most were skilled cowboys by their late teens and were already well into their life's work. Miguel Muñiz was an example: "I began learning and was a good cowboy by age twenty," he said. Those who would not become vaqueros learned the dozens of other jobs the ranches needed to make their operations successful.

The first day a boy rode with his father was a rite of passage. The youngster had prepared for this day all his life, since the time he began riding his stick horse just after learning to walk. The boy's growing excitement was soon mixed with gnawing apprehension as he readied himself for his first test in the cow camp. Expert vaqueros would be watching closely. If he passed, if he had practiced enough and had learned acceptable skills as a roper and rider, he knew that by age sixteen he might be allowed to participate in the summer roundups and go on the payroll. If he failed . . . but that was unthinkable. Rogerio Silva told about his first day:

> My brother-in-law, Venuseriano "Niñe" Quintanilla, was the boss, and he made sure I got a fully trained horse from the *remuda* [group of horses used to work cattle]. He knew that King Ranch Quarter Horses would do most of the work for the rider. When I made a mistake, Niñe called me aside for further instruction so as not to embarrass me in front of the other men. Then he said, "Watch me," and demonstrated the proper way to cut the cow, rope the calf, or whatever skill he was showing me.

Each girl had a rite of passage, too. It was on her fifteenth birthday. A celebration, called a *quinceañera*, marked her coming of age. In earlier times, the quinceañera was a minor church celebration. The girl's family might have a simple celebration at home afterward with close family members present. After World War II (1941–1945), the families had more money and could better afford a more elaborate quinceañera. Quinceañeras are still common today.

An honoree may have as many as fourteen of her friends and their escorts in her presentation. She will likely wear a fancy white ball gown and a tiara in her hair. Her girl friends usually wear matching white dresses, and the boys wear tuxedos or, occasionally, jeans with white shirts. The two to five hundred guests at these large quinceañeras, including many relatives, sip punch and eat cake and sometimes dinner. Around 9:00 P.M., the master of ceremonies formally presents the honoree and her attendants to the guests; then dancing lasts until midnight. Some guests bring the honoree gifts, usually money in amounts ranging from $10 to $20.

Girls followed after their mothers and learned girl jobs from them in much the same way as boys learned boy jobs from their fathers. They learned to wash, iron, chop wood, sew, and cook. In the early 1900s, Manuela Mayorga helped her mother, Antonia Cavazos, and her grandmother, Virginia Cavazos, prepare special meals for guests at King Ranch. They used their family recipe to make tamales from rabbits the men killed on the Ranch. They also made big tubs of beef enchiladas. Since Manuela's house was across

1984 - 1999
Mis Quince Años

Mr. and Mrs. Joe T. Garcia
request the honor of your presence
at the Quinceañera of their daughter

Samantha Jo Garcia

on Saturday, the twenty-eighth of August
Nineteen hundred and ninety-nine
at five o'clock p.m.

St. Gertrude Catholic Church
Corner of 8th and Caesar, Kingville, Texas

Dinner and Dance
following at the KC Hall
320 E. General Cavazos Blvd.

Dance 9 p.m. - 1 a.m.
Music by
Hi Tech Sounds Leo Saenz

An invitation to the quinceañera celebration of Samantha Jo García.

Family working in a cotton field. *Photo by Sue Ford. Photo courtesy of the South Texas Archives, Jernigan Library, Texas A&M University–Kingsville.*

the street from the school, she often didn't get to play at recess, but had to go home to help grind corn for the tortillas. Manuela also added to the family income by helping her father pick cotton. She liked going to work with him, even when they had to leave at 4:00 A.M. to walk to the cotton fields. Manuela was fast and, by 5:00 in the afternoon, she could pick two hundred pounds of cotton. She earned $1.25 for each one hundred pounds she picked.

The stable, secure lifestyle of the Ranches could not always shield youngsters from family tragedy. But, without fail, other families, usually relatives, took care of children if their parents died. When Juan Guevara Sr. was a young boy, his mother became seriously ill with tuberculosis. He and his sister helped her with the household chores and took care of her as best they

Juan Guevara Sr. is a retired third-generation vaquero on Kenedy Ranch.

Manuela Mayorga helped her mother, Antonia Gaytan, and her grandmother, Virginia Cavazos, make enchiladas for Mrs. Henrietta King. Manuela also picked cotton in the fields with her father for extra money.

Antonia Cavazos Gaytan worked for Mrs. Henrietta King and helped prepare enchiladas for her and her guests.

Photograph by Toni Frissell. Copyright © King Ranch, Inc., Kingsville, Texas.

could. Juan said, "We gave her anise [an herb] tea to help her cough. When she died, my sister and I made candy to sell at the Ranch to make money. We would heat one quart of Pet milk and two cups of sugar and boil it. We stirred and stirred and poured it into a pan, and it would set. Then we would slice it and sell it for one cent a piece." Juan and his sister lived with an aunt after their mother's death.

Teresa Mayorga grew up on King Ranch in the 1920s. Her mother was dead, so an aunt and uncle took care of her. Her father was the famous vaquero Macario Mayorga of the Kenedy, King, and East Ranches. He competed in rodeos all over Texas and Mexico representing the Ranches, so he was often away from home. Teresa's eyes lit up when she remembered: "My father would return home bringing clothes for me wrapped in his yellow slicker on the back of his horse. He brought presents. He brought his check of the past months to help pay my way [food and clothing]."

*   *   *

The sons and daughters of the Wild Horse Desert grew up with a strict personal code stemming from a proud tradition. Generation after generation of these young people developed into the dedicated, highly specialized, loyal work force that has enabled the Ranches to operate with little disruption ever since the late 1850s and 1860s when Captain Richard King and his friend, Captain Mifflin Kenedy, began their great ranching ventures. The close family unit was one of the main reasons for their success.

CHAPTER THREE

The Family Was First

Kineño and Kenedeño families valued a stable, dependable, predictable family tradition above all else. Each member knew exactly what was expected of him or her by the other family members and by the employers. The father was the undisputed head of the family and as such was the provider, disciplinarian, and business manager. He usually did all the shopping, drove the car if there was one, and paid the bills. His wife stayed close to home and was in command of the household. She tended to the family's day-to-day needs, such as food and laundry. She sewed all of the family's clothing, except for shoes and hats. The mother was in charge of the family's—and sometimes the neighbors'—health and medicinal remedies, including birthings. And she was responsible for religious training, celebrations, and funerals.

Every day the mother was up first, building a fire in the wood stove and putting on a pot of beans to boil for lunch or dinner. She prepared breakfast, usually eggs, potatoes, and fresh tortillas. Beef was always part of the family diet, and sometimes there were other specialties. Stella Guevara on Kenedy Ranch said her family also ate rabbits, javelina, and wild duck. She said, "Daddy loved armadillo. We cleaned and washed it. Rubbed it with chili powder, cov-

STELLA GUEVARA'S ARMADILLO RECIPE

Clean (skin) the armadillo.

Wash the armadillo.

Rub the armadillo with chili powder.

Place the armadillo in a pan, cover with foil and bake two or three hours.

ered with foil, baked slow two or three hours. Used chili powder to kill the taste of javelina. We steamed it."

All the family's clothes were sewn by hand at first, and then sewing machines came in around 1915. Enemorio Serna, born in 1931, said his mother bought bolts of material at the Ranch Commissary to make all the pants, shirts, and dresses for her nine children. He laughed, "One time she forgot to put a fly in my pair of pants, and I had to hurry and cut a hole with a knife—it was funny."

Women had very little social life and rarely went away from home, though they occasionally gathered to visit and do needlework when the men were working in the cow camps. Dora Maldonado, Beto's wife, said, "I've been here forty-six years, and I went to the Commissary once. Beto did the shopping. He's the boss and he's been the boss, and he buys. He does everything . . . If I need something, I just tell Beto."

Women understood and accepted that men were head of the family. Women were the great silent partners of the husband-wife partnership. However, when the men were gone for weeks at a time on the range, the women were quite capable of taking care of the family. Rogerio Silva said, "Mom raised the family. She chopped wood, milked cows, fed chickens, turkeys, and did the garden. Mom also whipped." Enemorio Serna on Kenedy Ranch was impressed by how hard his mother worked:

> My mother believed you were somebody if you were clean and so we were scrubbed every day using the same soap made from tallow and lye used for the clothes. It was made from a recipe handed down from her mother. There were nine children, and it took until midnight to bathe and put us all to bed. Then she was up again before daylight to begin cooking the day's food. You wonder when the lady slept.

Enemorio also said his mother was a good shot and used her gun to kill snakes.

In their husbands' absence, women also dealt with emergencies as they arose. When Valentín Quintanilla Jr. was ten years old, his father was out working on the windmills when his mother, Elesa, looked up and saw a big storm coming. She quickly gathered her seven children and started for safety. When they were less than a hundred yards away from their house, they watched in shock as the storm totally destroyed their home. It also blew off the roof of the barn, leaving only the metal supports. Fighting a drowning rain, the ranch hands tugged and strained until they pulled huge tarpaulins across the supports. Elesa huddled with her children and the ranch hands from 1:00 P.M. to 6:00 A.M. the next morning as they rode out the storm, not knowing if her husband was alive or dead. All of them sur-vived, and the Ranch relocated them in another house on the Ranch. Help from the Ranch after losing everything they owned is an example of why workers were content to remain on the Ranches.

*   *   *

In the early days on the Ranches, marriages were sometimes performed by one of the Ranch bosses, since there were no priests or churches near by. Valentín Quintanilla Jr. and his wife were married in 1930 by Larry Cavazos, foreman on King Ranch, then were re-married when the priest came. Priests came to the Ranches only two to four times a year to conduct Mass, marriages, baptisms, and hear confessions. Later, in the 1940s and 1950s, some families owned cars and transportation became much easier. When some couples de-cided to get married, they went to town for a simple ceremony and returned home for chocolate and cookies with their family. Other couples had an elabo-rate ceremony and invited many of their

Valentín Quintanilla Sr. and his wife, Elesa Pérez Quintanilla. A hurricane hit King Ranch while Valentín was away, and Elesa barely got their children out of their house before it was blown away.

friends and family members for a big celebration. These couples were expected to follow a fairly strict set of rules.

When one of these couples from the Kineño and Kenedeño families decided to marry, their next step was usually much more complicated than just shopping for an engagement ring. A third person called a *postadores* would act as a go-between for the two families to find out if the girl's parents would give permission for the marriage. Manuela Mayorga told about this custom:

Couples would meet at a dance. The young man would decide he wanted to marry and would tell his father. The father arranged for a *postadores* to pay a visit to the girl's family. Sometimes a respected member of the family would do this duty. The girl's family usually didn't know the suitor until the *postadores* told them. The *postadores* made two visits. He asked for the girl's hand in marriage on the first visit. The girl's family would tell the postadores to come back in fifteen days for an answer if the answer was to be affirmative. If the answer was negative, the *postadores* was told to come back in eight days. Fifteen days meant yes; eight days meant no.

If the parents approved, they began planning for the wedding celebration, which customarily included plenty of food, music, and dancing. Some families allowed no dating between the time of the engagement and the wedding. Manuela Mayorga told of her daughter's courtship: "On May 10 was the first visit. The wedding date was set for September 20. She couldn't talk to him. She had to sneak around at church. She would take flowers to the trash to sneak out and talk to him. There was no dating except to sneak out."

Women preparing for a wedding feast. *Photo by Sue Ford. Photo courtesy of the South Texas Archives, Jernigan Library, Texas A&M University–Kingsville.*

The two sets of parents set the date and made all of the decisions about the wedding, usually about a month ahead of time. The parents shared the expenses. The couple usually married in the church on Saturday, sometimes at morning Mass. Typically, there followed a reception, lunch at noon, and supper that night before the dance that could last until midnight or daylight. The jubilant crowd danced to waltzes, polkas, and Mexican dances such as *paso doble, cuadrillas, dansa loches,* and *el ocho.* Music was played on accordions, guitars, flutes, and violins. Before 1900, the dance would last for several days.

Following the wedding ceremony, the couple expected to live with one set of parents until they got housing of their own. If they proved their skill, hard work, and loyalty for a year or more, they would get their own house when one became available. The first houses on the Wild Horse Desert were *jacales,* crudely made huts of mesquite poles, grass, and mud with dirt floors which were common when Captain King established his *rancho* in 1854. He and his bride, Henrietta, began their life together in a *jacal.* Kineños and Kenedeños constructed these *jacales,* then later built wood-frame houses on both Ranches. The Ranches furnished housing for the workers as part of their salaries.

Plácido L. Maldonado and his sisters in front of their home, which was provided by King Ranch.

Nicolasa Quintanilla García and José García on their wedding day, February 12, 1949.

Often the King and Kenedy Ranch owners participated in workers' family weddings as guests or by giving gifts or money or maybe by furnishing a large cow for the customary barbecue. Nicolasa Quintanilla García described her wedding:

> After the wedding, we all went to my house, and I changed into a beige suit—a casual suit—and had punch, coffee, and cookies. They served lunch, which was *carne asada* [barbecue] and potato salad and *cabrito* [goat] for about a hundred people. The Ranch gave us the meat. Then there was a dance at 7:00, and it lasted until 12:00. The wedding date was February 12, 1949. We went to the Ricardo Hotel in town (Kingsville) for our honeymoon night. Our presents were dishes, sheets, bowls, and things like that. We lived with my mother.

All celebrations related to the church in some way. In addition to weddings, Christmas and baptisms were special occasions. By far the hap-

Martín Mendietta Jr., his wife, and their nine sons at a Christmas party at King Ranch where each boy received a toy truck. Eight of these boys became vaqueros like their father and grandfather, Martín Mendietta Sr.

piest times were at Christmas. It was the only time of the year ranch worker families received gifts. They did not celebrate birthdays until recently, as there was little or no money for presents. The men had their only vacation of the year from Christmas until after New Year's Day, and this made the season even more fun. Special foods prepared for the holidays were tamales and *buñuelos*, fried, puffed tortillas sprinkled with sugar and cinnamon. These sweet-smelling *buñuelos* were often piled on plates and taken to neighbors as gifts during holiday visits.

Sometimes the Kineños and Kenedeños put on plays with religious themes during the Christmas season, usually in the school building. Plácido L. Maldonado said, "We had a Christmas play called *Las Pastorelas*. It was a play about a shepherd and a devil who visit the baby Jesus. It lasted from 6:00 P.M. Christmas Eve to 1:00 or 2:00 A.M. There were twelve shepherds, three devils, an angel, La Aile, Bartolo, and a chorus."

Workers' families did not have much money to spend at Christmas time, but they always had special foods. Manuela Mayorga could still remember: "On Christmas Day, we had lots of tamales. We had gifts at home, but they were little because we didn't have any money. Gifts were made sometimes." Celebrations for the ranch workers' families were held by both ranches and were an important part of the workers' Christmas holidays.

Antonio Salinas told about Christmas on Kenedy Ranch: "The big oak tree at the Big House was the Christmas tree. We would all gather there, and [John Gregory] Kenedy [Sr.] would come and bring fruit, candies, gifts."

Beto Maldonado's dad, Librado, played Santa Claus for years on King Ranch. The children would gather at the Christmas tree, and "Santa Claus" would pass out presents to each child. Librado's Santa suit and voice were so believable the children would not recognize him. Beto said, "Everybody got gifts. Wives [got] blankets, pillow cases, sheets. Men got gloves, jackets. Kids got a present and a bag of fruit, candy, and nuts."

Manuel Silva's family had a dance with food piled high at Christmas. They had to kill two cows to feed everyone.

There were no churches on the Ranches, and priests rode their horses there to hold church services and religious celebrations only a few times a year. This left the responsibility for the daily training of the children in church teachings and rituals to the women. These lessons usually took place in front of altars in homes. Gavina Mendietta's altar was typical. It included a cloth, handmade candles, a picture of the Virgin Mary, a statue of Saint Guadalupe (Our Lady of Guadalupe), a cross, and handmade crepe-paper flowers in shades of brilliant orange, red, yellow, green, and pink. "I said the rosary every night before the altar with [my] children kneeling," said Gavina. "At Christmas, I put moon and stars above the altar. My mother had a small cradle with baby Jesus on the altar at Christmas."

Religious rituals were always special occasions marked by the gathering of friends and family to visit and share special foods. Parents always selected godparents for their children's baptisms, confirmations, and first communions. Many times they chose different ones, often relatives, for each event. Sometimes they chose more prosperous members of the community, since raising a child could be very expensive. Godparents understood that they would be responsible for the child if its parents died, even if family members took the child in. Godparents took their role seriously. Godparents, their godchild, and the godchild's parents developed a close, special relationship.

A nun visits the school on the Norias Division of King Ranch. The school also served as a church when a priest or nuns came to visit. *Photograph by Toni Frissell. Copyright © King Ranch, Inc., Kingsville, Texas.*

A visit by nuns to the Norias Division of King Ranch. *Courtesy King Ranch Archives, King Ranch, Inc., Kingsville, Texas.*

The celebration of Ryann Gonzales's first communion. Pictured are (from left) Ricardo Longoria, Father Angel Villalha, Ryann, and Josefina Longoria.

No doctors or nurses lived on the Ranches. Doctors were called to the Ranch or patients taken to the doctor in Kingsville only for extremely critical illness or injury. Women took care of most medical needs on the Ranches. They took care of two kinds of needs. First, they treated colds, flu, fever, headaches, upset stomachs, and minor infections using herb cures handed down through their families. Nicolas Rodríguez said, "We had an herb that was called the *comanche*, which was used for fevers. The herb was cut, smashed, and put in clean water. The water would turn purple, and then a cup or two would be given to the babies or the one who had fever. That would be enough to cut the fever." The Seferino Gutiérrez family on Kenedy Ranch used kerosene mixed with three teaspoons of sugar, then marked with a cross on the forehead, for colds and snake bites. Snake bites were also treated by sticking a dagger plant around the bite, then pouring on kerosene. The women rubbed a match on spider bites to stop the pain and boiled the peel of an *amarosa* plant to ease stomach aches.

> The Seferino Gutiérrez family on Kenedy Ranch used kerosene mixed with three teaspoons of sugar, then marked with a cross on the forehead, for colds and snake bites.

The women's second responsibility was helping with the birthing of babies. *Parteras* (midwives) delivered nearly all babies. Doctors were hardly ever involved.

In the early days, there were no funeral homes on the Wild Horse Desert. Family members died at home and were buried the next day. The women carefully washed the body and prepared it for burial. Stella Guevara on Kenedy Ranch said that when Teresa Mayorga Cuellar's grandmother died, they put cotton in her ears and nose. This preparation usually took place outside in back of the house. The body was then placed on a board, table, or bed in the house. Sometimes candles were burned in the room, and if the weather was hot, ice was placed on the floor underneath the body. Neighbors brought food, and some of them sat up all night with the body, visiting with family members. Funeral customs were similar for both the ranch workers and the ranch owner families.

Enemorio "Tequito" Serna talked about these customs:

When somebody died, they bought the box [coffin]. They held the funeral the next day. The body was kept at home. Everyone came and brought food. The women wore black from head to toe, including the veil. Some wore it a year. My aunt for the rest of her life.

Ofelia M. Longoria said, "When my aunt died, they laid her out at the house and stayed up with her all night. My grandmother gave the rosary. The priest came for the burial."

A funeral home for both Anglos and Mexicans was finally established in Kingsville in about 1953. It was located in the Allen Furniture Store. Clyde M. Allen Jr., present owner of the store, told how the funeral home worked:

> A chapel and embalming room were located in the furniture store, and they also sold caskets and burial supplies. They had a hearse in the 1920s that was drawn by four white horses. Later, they had motor hearses that were kept in the garage next door. The people who worked in the furniture store also dug the graves and drove the hearse.

Family members were close and provided support for each other from birth until death. They celebrated together and grieved together, and the ranching community was their extended family.

CHAPTER FOUR

How It All Happened

Julián Buentello began his long career as a vaquero on King Ranch by rounding up Longhorn cattle. He saw them disappear from being the main stock of South Texas, then finally return in the 1950s to continue their long, colorful history.

These magnificent animals had a majestic stature and horns that could grow to an average of four feet. They first roamed these grasslands when the Spanish *conquistadores* explored what is now Texas and left them behind in the 1500s. These animals became known as Texas Longhorns. They were tough and could thrive in the hot, dry Wild Horse Desert, but they were not very good to eat. Eventually they were killed mainly for their hides and tallow (fat) to sell to merchants in the eastern United States for such uses as making candles. Large factories for rendering tallow were built on the big ranches, and the hides and tallow were shipped by boat from Corpus Christi to the East Coast.

After the American Civil War (1861–1865), the country was hungry for meat. The Kings and Kenedys had been mixing better cattle with theirs to produce better table meat. José Morales and Guadalupe Morales picked up

A Texas Longhorn on King Ranch.

Photo by Betty Bailey Colley.

some of the better breeds of cattle and brought them to Kenedy Ranch in carts. Eventually the Longhorns were phased out. Guadalupe Morales told about the upbreeding on Kenedy Ranch: "They brought in white-faced cattle, but they did not work out . . . eventually they brought in 'red cattle' and Brahmas and slowly got rid of the Mexican cattle [Longhorns]."

The King and Kenedy Ranches now had good table beef for the nation, but they had a problem. Trains had not come to South Texas yet. How could the ranchers get their cattle to market? It was a thousand miles from the Ranches to the railroads in the Midwest where beef cattle could be shipped east to market. The answer was the great trail drives of the 1870s and 1880s. Julián and his wife Antonia Buentello heard stories from their family members about these trail rides. When cattle were to be driven up the trail, Julián said his father told him that there were pastures with pens in them, and all the cattle from surrounding ranches would be herded and held there. One time, lightning struck and killed many of the cattle before they could even start the drive. These gatherings were in holding pens called *partidas,* and once the cattle were in place, the decision would be made as to which cattle would go up the trail, which would be slaughtered, and which were to be sent back to the ranches.

Antonia said her father also told her about the drives:

> He said they would have to herd the cattle at night to keep them together. They worked shifts. All the cattlemen would bring their cattle to the *partidas* on the Ranch.

Ranchers could make a great deal of money once their cattle were moved up the trail from Texas to towns like Sedalia, Missouri, and Abilene and Dodge City, Kansas. Cattle that were worth $11 in Texas could be sold in Abilene for $22 and then at the slaughterhouses in Chicago for $44. During this time, records show that 5,800,000 cattle, 1,000,000 horses, and 35,000 men went up the trails. This business made a good profit until around 1885, when barbed wire was invented. Settlers began building fences around their land with the new wire. They closed the open ranges and ended the trail drives forever. It was a good thing when railroads finally reached South Texas and could be used to move cattle to market. After the trail drives had ended and railroads were built, the vaqueros' work continued on the huge pastures of the King and Kenedy Ranches, rounding up and branding cattle.

Trail drives required brave men. There were no roads, only danger all along the way through uncivilized and partly unexplored territory. Lightning storms, stampedes, raging rivers, accidents, and robbers were just some of the challenges. In his thesis on Kenedy Ranch Roberto Villarreal wrote:

> One of the Kenedy crew of vaqueros was taking the cattle up the trail when they approached one of the many rivers to cross. Martín Acuña was pushing the cattle across the river when suddenly he and his horse disappeared under the water. The horse came up, but the vaquero did not.

Trail drives also required tough men with expert skills. Drives usually lasted from early spring to late summer. During the day, the vaqueros had to drive thousands of wild cattle from one point to another with-

TEXAS CATTLE TRAILS, 1870–1880S

Courtesy of Nancy Tiller

out losing or stampeding them. At night they took turns staying with the cattle so they would stay calm. They knew how to string the cattle out near a watering hole so about twenty could drink at a time. Otherwise, the cattle would all run to the water at once and trample each other, or maybe stampede. Dust was one of the biggest problems both at roundup and on the trail as the cowboys rode among thousands of cattle, all kicking up dirt that seeped into the men's mouths, ears, and noses. The vaqueros could have been mistaken for bandits with their wide-brimmed hats pulled low and their bandannas yanked up against the grit, leaving only a slit for their eyes. The men rotated sides depending on which way the wind was blowing. New hands were always sure to get the worst side.

Choosing men to entrust with such valuable herds along these trails was a big decision. Texas ranch owners worked Anglo, Black, and Hispanic cowboys on these trail drives, at least an eight- to twelve-week trip. Sometimes King and Kenedy hired private contractors to take the herds north, and at other times they chose Kenedy and King family members or Kenedeños and Kineños for this troublesome task. Allen Jones, a Black trail boss, also took herds up the Chisholm Trail.

José Alvarado is a descendant of Francisco Alvarado (born 1800), who died defending the King family during the American Civil War. José told how his grandfather, Ramón Alvarado, helped Francisco build the first *jacales* (houses made of mesquite poles, mud, and straw) in 1854. Ramón was also one of the first cow bosses and made many successful trips with herds to the North as trail boss in the 1870s. He had experience and was good at solving problems. Around 1882, King contracted with a man named North to take cattle up the trail. When the cattle stampeded and North lost control, King dispatched Ramón with his *remuda* by train to Corpus Christi. There the *remuda* and supply wagons were loaded on a train that took them to the cattle, and Ramón soon rounded up the cattle and took them up the trail.

It was during these drives that many of the tales of the Wild West were born. Some were based on truth, and some were born of the imagination of clever storytellers around campfires when the long, dusty day was spent and the cattle were finally quiet.

In his book, *Cow People*, J. Frank Dobie, a famous teller of cowboy tales, told a legendary story about the loyalty of the Alvarado family. His story of Ablos Alvarado illustrates Captain King's ultimate trust in the Kineños to bring the cattle safely up the trail.

According to Dobie's story, in the spring of 1880, King had a herd ready to go up the trail to Dodge City. Ablos was late. Three days passed. Still no Ablos. Young Richard King II was very impatient and wanted to know why his father, the Captain, was waiting on that old man. Finally, Ablos showed up, and he took charge of a herd worth thousands of dollars. Captain King and his son went on ahead to Kansas to await the herds. As the other trail bosses arrived in Kansas, the Captain would ask them how the trail had been. The first trail boss reported that he had had trouble at the Cimarron, and some of his cattle had drowned. The second trail boss replied that it had rained and stormed through the Indian territory, and he had lost some cattle in a stampede. Several days later Ablos arrived. Captain King asked him how his drive had been. He said, "Oh, *muy bien*, señor. No trouble at all. We came along *despacio, despacio*, slow, slow. I picked up 136 King Ranch cattle lost out of other herds. We are 136 cattle long. And look how the cattle have gained in weight! Look how contented they are!" Captain King turned to Richard and said, "Now you know why I wait for Ablos."

*   *   *

Felipe García enjoyed his work as a vaquero on King Ranch. But he knew, like all the other vaqueros, that the most important man on the ranch range or on the trail was the cook. The cook held a unique role, and a good cook was considered absolutely necessary to keep the men satis-

A camp scene around chuckwagons. *Copyright © King Ranch, Inc., Kingsville, Texas.*

fied. The cook also made more money than anyone else. Ramon F. Adams described the range cook in his book, *Come an' Get It*, like this:

> As a rule range cooks were a homely lot, possessing hair-trigger tempers, many of them being as quick with a gun as they were with a pothook. But the cook's word was law. The chuck wagon—and sixty feet around it—was under his absolute control. The roundup boss was careful to use diplomacy when giving orders around the wagon, and even the owner of the cattle walked softly there.

One day Felipe was offered the chance to become a cook if he could learn the necessary skills in thirty days. He decided to try. His teacher was an old cook, Holotino "La Chista" (little sparrow) Villarreal, a famous King Ranch cook for thirty years. He got his nickname because he hopped around like a little bird. He even had a small bird painted on his chuck wagon. Felipe knew that most chuck wagon cooks learned this way, by taking lessons from a "master cook," and he was eager to learn.

Felipe's first lesson from La Chista was one of his most important ones, how to make *pan de campo* (camp bread). These skillet-sized disks of bread were part of the vaqueros' diet, every day. Felipe said he had no recipe to follow, so he watched La Chista very carefully:

> La Chista knew just how much flour, baking powder, salt, milk, warm water, and shortening to add to get the bread just right. I had to learn to feel when the dough was the right consistency, to just know when the bread was done, brown on the bottom and on the top.

La Chista also taught Felipe how to build the fire and burn it down to just the right temperature and how to cook beans, rice, fried steak, and tortillas. After just two weeks, Felipe knew enough that he felt he could go it alone. He spent the rest of his days on the Ranch as a cook for the vaqueros. After he had been cooking for a while, he developed his own specialties of fried fruit pies, sweet breads like doughnuts, and both vanilla and chocolate cakes.

JUAN GUEVARA JR.'S RECIPE FOR *PAN DE CAMPO*

10 pounds flour

2 spoons baking powder

$1/2$ spoon sugar

2 cups Pet milk

4 spoons shortening (like Crisco)

Mix all together. Add $1/2$ quarts water. Let the mixture rise 10 or 15 minutes. Roll or pat out to $1/2$ inch thick to fit pan.

Cook 6 or 7 minutes over camp fire with hot coals heaped on the lid. Repeat until all the dough is cooked.

Felipe soon found out that the cook's duties went way beyond just cooking. He also learned that the chuck wagon was more than a portable place to cook.

Feeding a hungry crew of cowhands was a challenge on the trail. The long, difficult drives usually traveled across land miles from grocery stores or even farms with food to sell. The men had to have plenty of hearty food to work this physically demanding job. Traveling a trail for weeks at a time through unpopulated country demanded a way to carry food and other provisions between supply points. The Texas rancher Charles Goodnight is credited with devising the chuck wagon in 1866 for this purpose, and the chuck wagon became an important fixture of ranch life well into the 1990s.

The chuck wagon was the cook's kitchen on wheels and the cowboy's eating place. It was his home away from home, both on the trail and on the remote pastures of the ranches. It was also the center of activity after a hard day's work, when the men would sing or tell stories around the campfire, or just rest.

JOSÉ ALEGRÍA'S RECIPE FOR COW'S HEAD

"First I dug a large round hole and built a fire in it. I then skinned and dehorned the cow head, seasoned it with salt, pepper, and garlic, then wrapped it in a cloth, then a tow sack. I wet the whole package with water. When the fire had burned down to coals, some dirt was spread on the coals, then the cow's head was placed in, then more dirt and then more coals. The head cooked all night. The next morning the head was unwrapped and ready to eat."

FELIPE GARCÍA'S COFFEE RECIPE

$1/2$ cups coffee to $1/2$ pot of water

Boil 30 minutes until white smoke comes out of the top of the pot.

Add $3/4$ cup cold water to settle the grounds to the bottom of the pot.

The typical chuck wagon had a bed with bottom and side boards made of wood. Usually, there were metal bows bent up over the bed and fastened on either side. A wagon sheet, or tarpaulin, could be stretched across this metal frame for protection from the sun or rain. The wagon contained a chuck box for holding the cook's equipment. The rear wall sloped outward from top to bottom and was hinged at the bottom, so that when the wall was pulled down and supported with a heavy stick, it made a table on which the cook could prepare the food, like a portable kitchen counter.

Pulled by mules, the chuck wagon carried the food supply, the eating and cooking utensils, bedrolls, and tools for building fire trenches, horse shoeing, and any other need that was likely to arise. The cook was often the doctor and dentist, so the drawers might also contain such remedies as quinine to treat fever; calomel for easing stomach problems; liniment, a medicated liquid for rubbing on sore muscles or inflamed injuries; and kerosene, a thin oil made from petroleum and used for treating snake bites. Kerosene also came in handy as a fire starter when the wood was wet.

Felipe, like some other cooks, carried a needle and thread and mended the men's clothes if necessary. He said, "You had to be nice to me if you wanted your clothes repaired."

The men were sometimes too tired and would be hot-tempered, especially after weeks on the range and a long, hot day's work. Usually the cook was the mediator, the one who settled the argument. Sometimes he was also the "banker" and held the men's money for bets.

All four sides of Felipe's chuck wagon could be pulled down and propped up to make work places. It was designed for use on King Ranch and made by the men who built the fences. It had a tank in back that held 250 gallons of water, enough for one day. The men filled their canteens from it. This wagon has been used for thirty years or more on King Ranch.

Felipe told how he hated to see spring come because this meant that it was time to clean the chuck wagons and get them ready for spring roundup. He used buckets of ash, sand, and lye soap and scrubbed and scrubbed the wagons with a brush inside and out until they were spot-

CHUCK WAGON

Water barrel

Stake ropes

Wagon bed (holds bedrolls)

Bows for tarpaulin

Tool Box

Chuck box for food, cutlery, plates, etc.

Lid pulls down to make a table for preparing food

Courtesy of Nancy Tiller

less. When this smelly, messy job was finished, the wagons dried in the hot Texas sun and were then ready to be packed.

Often the camps would have two cooks and sometimes two chuck wagons if they were moving big herds spread out on the huge pastures of the Ranches. Cooks often had to prepare meals in a different place every day and were always on the move. While one cook stayed with the big chuck wagon at the main camp, the other cook hitched up a smaller wagon, loaded it with enough food to feed twenty to thirty men, and located a camp near trees, closer to the herd. Here he would throw up a tarpaulin for shade, build a mesquite fire, start the coffee, beans, and rice boiling, dress the fresh beef that had been killed earlier that morning, and begin preparing *pan de campo*.

Jesús Gonzales was apprenticed as a cook as a young boy on Kenedy Ranch. He began by washing dishes for the cook and soon learned the techniques and recipes of the range:

> The chuck wagon was wooden and had wooden wheels with metal spokes. Mules pulled it. We traveled about ten or fifteen miles a day from the camp to the roundup site. It took one-and-a-half or two hours to get there. We washed dishes in hot water and [used] bar soap. We made wood fires and used kerosene to start them.
>
> I got up at 3:00 or 4:00 to cook breakfast of refried beans, coffee, and bread. For lunch, we cooked beans, rice, fried meat, bread, and coffee. I fed twenty-five [vaqueros] at a time.

Days on the range were not always without fun. The vaqueros liked to play jokes on each other. The cook especially attracted kidding from the crew. Vaqueros liked to tell a story about one day when La Chista was moving through a pasture in a truck with the chuck wagon tied on behind it. He was on his way to set up for the noon meal. The vaqueros started waving frantically and yelling at him and trying to get him to stop. He just kept waving back and was not about to stop because they were always playing jokes on him. La Chista had lost his chuck wagon and it wasn't until several miles later that he turned around and realized that his chuck wagon was nowhere in sight. He had to go back to get it and put up with a lot of teasing.

The cook totally controlled what happened around the chuck wagon at mealtime. The cowboy selected a plate, cup, knife, and fork from the chuck box at the wagon, then went from pot to skillet and helped himself to food and coffee. The dining table was anywhere the cowboy could find a place big and clean enough to squat or sit. He often sat cross-legged, using the calves of his legs to balance his plate while his coffee cup sat on the ground. He could even cut his meat while sitting in this position. Sometimes his bedroll was his "table."

The cowboy's social etiquette on the King and Kenedy Ranches was very similar to that of other ranches and was strictly observed: Ramon Adams, in *Come an' Get It*, described a typical set of rules at mealtime:

1. The hands ate as they came in instead of waiting for everyone. It was more polite to go ahead and serve themselves than to have the others stand in line waiting.

2. Even if everyone was there at once, there was no crowding, shoving, rushing, or reaching in front of another man. These were not allowed.

3. The Dutch oven lids were kept away from the sand, and the cowboys had to be careful to put the lids back on the pots and the pots back on the fire so that the food would be hot for those still to come.

4. A cowboy did not take the last serving unless he was sure everyone else was finished eating.

5. There was no waste. The cowboy left no food on his plate. He either ate all the food or scraped it off for the animals and birds to eat. He might put it in a can for leftovers that would be fed to animals later. He would then place his dirty dishes in the huge dishpan for washing.

6. It was bad manners to tie a horse to a wheel of the chuck wagon, or to ride into camp so that the wind blew sand in the food the cook was preparing.

7. The men dared not eat until the cook called it ready.

8. If he found the water barrel empty, the cowhand's duty was to fill it.

9. Leaving the bedroll unrolled and out of place was against the rules. This might cause it to be "accidentally" left behind when the cook packed up.

10. Around the campfire, an unwritten law was that a song or fiddle piece or story was not interrupted.

11. A stranger would always be welcome at the wagon and ate with the cowhands. The unwritten code was that he was expected to dry the dishes.

Usually, the important meal of the day at camp was supper. While breakfast and lunch were hurried, the evening meal could be more relaxed. This was the time when the men could sit down and eat and spin yarns around the campfire, and maybe hear one of the hands sing or play a little music. Other nights they just rested until bedtime and thought of their families at home. During this time, the cook cleaned up his "kitchen," washed the dishes, and made preparations for the next day's meals.

After World War II, when the roads were black-topped, the ranches built camp houses in some of the big pastures. Camp houses on King Ranch were made of concrete blocks. The ones on Kenedy Ranch were made mostly of wood from spruce trees, but some were made of concrete. Here the men could sleep and have their breakfast and supper prepared. Chuck wagons were still used to provide the noon meal out on the range where the men were working.

Cooks were usually men; Ofelia M. Longoria on King Ranch was an exception. She had a job as a cook at one of the camp houses, where she fed as many as ninety men in a day. She said:

> As far as I know, I was the only woman to ever serve as a regular cook for the men working the Ranches. Bobby Cavazos hired me. He told me the men would respect me . . . I had a face like a lemon.

She was about forty years old when she started this job and worked for seventeen years, from 1966 until about 1983. She described her routine:

> I had two gas stoves, and one person helped me at breakfast, and one helped at lunch. I got to the camp house at 3:00 A.M. I made tortillas in the morning and camp bread at noon. In the morning I served French fries, eggs, chorizo [spicy sausage], tortillas, coffee, and tea.
>
> Breakfast was served at 6:30. I went home to rest for about an hour before lunch.
>
> I served lunch at 12:00. I served *carne guisada* [beef stew], rice, beans, camp bread, Kool-Aid, and tea. After lunch I took a siesta.
>
> Supper was at 5:30. I would rotate serving meat and stew between lunch and dinner. I also served camp bread, tea, and Kool-Aid. It took a half-sack of flour to make the seven or eight rounds of camp bread for each meal.

Ofelia Longoria said she was the only woman camp cook she knew of on King Ranch. She cooked for as many as ninety men a day.

The men would steal my tortillas and take them with them. I would hear them talking on the radio about eating them and how good they were.

My first camp boss was Reynaldo [her husband], and then Felix. I got a week off for vacation and was paid $600 a month. I started learning to cook when I was ten [years old].

By 1995, the routine feeding of the men in the King and Kenedy cow camps and camp houses had ceased. The delicious smells of fresh beef, camp bread, and steaming black coffee over open fires were history. The men now either take their lunches or drive their pickups into town for hamburgers and fries or drop by a Mexican restaurant. Some of the chuck wagons are in museums and are brought out only on special occasions to celebrate the life of the cowboy on the open range. Stories are still told of the important role the chuck wagon played in the development of the cattle industry in the United States.

Many American cowboy traditions were born during the time of roundups from horseback and the great trail drives. Julián and Antonia Buentello, Felipe García, Jesús Gonzales, La Chista Villarreal, Ofelia Longoria, and José and Guadalupe Morales kept these traditions and added their own for future generations.

CHAPTER FIVE

Round 'Em Up, Move 'Em Out

George Mayorga had his own way of soothing a bawling, restless sea of cattle during roundups. George loved to sing and play his harmonica, and music would quiet the bawling, milling cattle at night. It seemed to calm them. George taught himself to play. Sometimes he played and sang songs such as "Stila Song," "The Purple Bull," or "El Rancho Grande" around the chuck wagon after supper. The hands liked to hear his music while they rested after a long, backbreaking day in the saddle. George's father, a vaquero before him, also played the harmonica. He bought one especially for George. That harmonica was one of George's prized possessions. He had already handed it down to his son when he told his story at the age of eighty-four.

These four vaqueros worked together for 48 years on King Ranch. They are (from left) Roberto Mendietta, Julián Buentello, Valentín Quintanilla Jr., and George Mayorga.

Before the vaqueros could work the cattle in the Wild Horse Desert, they had to find, or "round up," these wild, stubborn animals. Their job was to bring them to a pasture where they would be divided. Some would begin the long trail to market or, later, to shipping pens near the railroad; others would go to the Ranch Headquarters for breeding. Rounding up cattle was the vaqueros' most important task. It was also their most difficult.

Vaqueros had to have unusual skills at roundup. They rode horseback through miles and miles of thick, scratchy brush to find the cattle. Vaqueros had to learn to actually "think like a cow" to locate them in the big pastures. King Ranch (1,300 square miles) alone is as large as the state of Rhode Island (1,231 square miles), with huge pastures. The largest pasture is 60,000 acres. Each pasture has its own name. The *corrida*, the basic work unit of fifteen to twenty cowboys, would spend a week or more riding the sand dunes, or looking for cattle under mesquite, in oak mottes (small groups of trees), and behind prickly pear cactus from dawn until dark. They wanted to find and bring in every last member of the herd. Enemorio Serna of Kenedy Ranch explained how hard it was to bring in some of the stubborn cows hiding in the thick brush:

Enemorio "Tequito" Serna was a vaquero on King Ranch nicknamed Tequito (Little Tick) because of his ability as a child to grab on to a horse and not let go.

> You couldn't see them, so you would have to track them. Sometimes you would have to get off your horse and lead him. You would rope the cow and tie it to a tree overnight. Then you would bring an ox in and tie the cow to the ox, and the ox would take it to the herd.

Cattle sometimes played games with the vaqueros. Some of the older, smarter cows knew how to hide and would lie down in thickets or low places until the vaqueros had passed. Vaqueros had to be smart to outwit these animals and round them up. These contests usually occurred twice a year, in fall and spring. Unless vaqueros had excellent horses and were very good at lassoing, they were sure to lose the battle. They knew that no animals were to be left behind during roundup. These animals were the same as dollars on the hoof. Also, the vaqueros wanted to do a good job. They worked extra hard to see that every animal was brought in and the roundup was complete.

One fact was in the vaqueros' favor. Cattle form cliques, not unlike those of teenagers. Cattle usually belong to a small group and stay together away from the others. They water together in the same place every day. The cattle clique has an older cow or steer as its leader. If one of these groups of cattle could be found drinking at one of the circular cement watering "ponds," every member of that group could be corralled into a holding pen. Vaqueros knew how to spot lead steers and get their help, because cattle would follow these steers into the pen.

Enemorio Serna of Kenedy Ranch describes his work at roundups:

> We brought Mexican steers—Longhorns—from near Rio Grande City to the Kenedy Ranch. Mexican Longhorns are smaller and meaner [than most cattle]. It took a week. We used two or three horses a day. There were two hundred horses in the *remuda*.
>
> Sometimes we had camp set up, sometimes we slept in the open. We used pens built along the way.
>
> A group of vaqueros went ahead and got permission to cross the plains and use water wells and holes. We would string them [the cattle] out and water about twenty at a time. The cattle ate grass on the trail. We would stop every two or three hours to graze them. The dust was bad. We used bandannas and rotated sides for the wind. New guys got the bad side.
>
> The Ranch furnished all our equipment. My father had to buy all of his. He was paid $.75 a day. It was in the 1930s in the Depression and it was [considered] a good job. Housing, food, and school were free.

Julián Buentello, of King Ranch, described what happened once cattle were gathered in one pasture:

When we got ready to round up a pasture, we would start off at a fast lope and drop the men off around the cattle in a big circle. When they were all in place we would holler one to the other, and then we would start running the cattle into the wind because it was cooler. It would take most of the morning. Then the men with the lead steers would rope them, and the rest would follow us to the pens, or to the rest of the herd. We would then cut the cattle out and drive those to the shipping pens that were going to be shipped.

During a large roundup, we would have to ride the herds at night to keep them calm. We would take the cattle to holding traps and work until the pasture was clear. Then we would send a message to the boss that the cattle were ready. He would come and we would cut the cattle.

Often two or three dogs worked roundups with the *corrida*. They were especially helpful to vaqueros faced with tracking stray cattle in thick brush. They could follow the scent for a quarter of a mile as much as a day after an "escape." One of these dogs was specially trained. When the vaquero called her name, she stood on her hind legs so the vaquero could grab her and lift her onto his horse. Then he could take her to the place where she would begin tracking the lost steer. This dog slept next to the cook, who got up at 3:00 A.M. every day. It was the dog who shook his bed to wake him. The cook began his day by petting the dog for a while, then preparing her food before starting breakfast for the hands.

"Cuando estábamos listos para rodear el ganado vacuno en una dehesa, empezábamos corriendo al rededor de la manada a paso largo y dejábamos a los vaqueros a varios puntos en un círculo grande rodeando la manada. Cuando todos estában en sus lugares, nos gritábamos uno al otro, y entonces empezamos a correr el ganado hacia el viento porque era mas fresco. Nos tomaba casi toda la mañana. Entonces los hombres enlazaban las reses quís, y los demás nos seguían al corral, o a donde estaba el resto de la manada. Entonces separábamos el ganado y arreábamos a los que se iban a mandar al mercado y los metíamos en el corral.

"Durante un rodeo grande, teníamos que montar toda la noche para que la manada se mantuviera tranquila. Llevábamos a la manada a unos corrales y continuábamos collectando reses hasta que habíamos limpiado la dehesa. Entonces le mandamos un mensaje al jefe que la manada estaba lista. El llegaba y cortamos las reses."

—Julián Buentello

After all of the cattle were rounded up, the next job was to cull, or remove, non-productive cows from the rest of the herd. When a cow went more than a year without bearing a calf, she was sold to market. These animals had to be spotted in a sea of sometimes 450 bawling, moving cattle raising dust in circles around the vaqueros. The caporal or owner spotted the animal that needed to be removed, and a vaquero would "cut" and begin moving it toward the outside of the circle, sometimes by force. The cow would then be picked up by another rider farther out on the edge of the circle of milling cattle and finally moved to an outrider, who would bring her to a group of lead steers. The steers would lead the cows to the pen. Another cull would have already been selected and be on the way out. This procedure would be repeated until all the less desirable cattle were cut from the main herd. According to Miguel Muñiz of King Ranch, "We would cut seven or eight hundred head of cattle from seven or eight thousand."

KING/KENEDY BRANDS
(see Appendix 2 for more brands)

King Ranch Brand—Running W.
Courtesy King Ranch Archives, King Ranch, Inc., Kingsville, Texas.

Kenedy Ranch Brand—Laurel Leaf.
Courtesy of the John G. and Marie Stella Kenedy Memorial Foundation.

The same technique was used for cutting cattle to go up the trail or for breeding at Ranch Headquarters. With the culling and cutting finally done, the cowboys were ready for the tedious job of branding the calves.

Vaqueros were expert at branding. As on most ranches, branding—or burning the ranch's mark on the animal with hot irons—was the practice used to identify cattle on the King and Kenedy Ranches. This method is still used today using electric branding irons. Young calves are numbered and marked when they weigh about 150 pounds. In the early days before fencing, this was absolutely necessary for record keeping in the breeding programs and for claiming cattle that might have strayed with other herds. Markings and brands also helped to recover cattle stolen by rustlers.

One vaquero expertly roped and threw the target calf while another vaquero branded it. Then men from the fence and windmills crews, who were called in to help with roundups, quickly brushed a mixture of lime and grease or water on the new brand or any wound the animal might have.

Nicolas Rodríguez said, "I knew when the iron was ready . . . it would turn red." Nicolas performed many tasks on King Ranch, but his specialty was branding. He knew just how to judge how long to leave the red-hot branding iron on the skin of the calf, long enough to leave a visible mark but not long enough to burn the flesh so that it was likely to become infected and endanger the animal's life. Nicolas said:

> I did all the branding myself because they trusted me very much. Whenever somebody else did the branding, the cattle's skin usually peeled off. I was very careful to make sure that the brand was just painted or stamped on the cattle, but not to burn them or hurt them. Sometimes, I got some help, because it was too much cattle, and I would get very tired.
>
> After branding the animal, one applied lime and water to cool off the burn. One had to be very careful not to burn the cattle when branding because they would bleed and get sick. The problem was that nobody could help me because Don Caesar [Kleberg] would not allow anybody else to do the job.

The owners on the King and Kenedy Ranches often worked closely with the roundups. Every animal meant investment and prospective profit or loss. There was also the element of wanting to be with the vaqueros to share in the results of their success. Often there was humor between owners and vaqueros. Richard "Dick" Kleberg Sr. (born 1887) was one of the owners who liked working alongside the vaqueros, and he was not above pulling a prank on them. He would choose a time when the camp was set up for lunch. When he thought the men were not paying attention, he would cut out a calf and send it running toward the camp. If the vaqueros were quick enough to rope the calf, they had fresh beef for lunch; if not, then they got beans and bread. Usually these expert ropers got their calf, and if they were close enough to home, they could take or send the leftover meat to their families.

The Kenedys also developed a close relationship with the workers on their ranch. Mifflin Kenedy's granddaughter, Sarita, and her brother, John G. Kenedy Jr., grew up speaking Spanish with the Kenedeño children and their families. Sarita was kind to the families of Ranch employees. After her father's death, she took the leadership in managing Kenedy Ranch with the help of the Kenedeños. She often worked alongside the men during roundup. Seferino Gutiérrez, expert roper and valued vaquero of Kenedy Ranch, said, "Sarita [Kenedy] East went on the range to supervise. She was a very good rider and helped cut the cattle. She was good people."

While the *corrida* was almost exclusively a man's world, there were some vaqueras, or cowgirls.

María Luisa Montalvo Silva was born into a family with a long, proud history on King Ranch. She grew up with a love of horses and had the opportunity to work side by side with the vaqueros as an equal. María said:

> I started working with Mr. Dick (Jr.) and Mr. Burwell in the *corrida* when I was about fourteen or fifteen. This was about 1940–1941. I was not afraid of anything, and loved working the cows. The men at the *corrida* would pick out a horse for me. The men were very respectful. My nickname was "Wicha." I held the cows during branding and helped bring them in. We would change horses about two or three times a day. I wore a bush jacket, chaps, men's boots, a hat, and spurs. I wore a handkerchief over my face. I remember how dusty it was when I was behind the cows. I remember having glasses on, and my face was solid dirt, and when I took off my glasses, my eyes were two white circles.

María Luisa Montalvo Silva grew up on the Laureles Division of King Ranch. She was one of the few women who worked with the men as a vaquera during roundups.

Josefina Robles Adrián, also of King Ranch, worked with her family out on a *ranchito* in the Big Caesar Pasture. *Ranchitos* were homesteads located in remote areas of the Ranch, usually near windmills, throughout the Ranch's vast acreage. As one of her chores, Josefina helped her father take care of cattle. She said that when her father died, the family was moved off the *ranchito* the next day because it was too dangerous for them to stay out there in a remote location by themselves without their father. There were no telephones or other means of communication to call for help in case of accidents, illness, attacks by wild animals, or cattle rustlers.

*   *   *

Vaqueros worked hard. "The work was tough—chasing wild cattle in the brush. Now everything hurts in the morning," explained Martín Mendietta Jr., of King Ranch.

The hours were long, and work often left little or no time for their families or anything else. Seferino Gutiérrez of Kenedy Ranch said, "We got up at 4:00, ate, saddled, and rode. Worked 'til dark with no breaks. Ate in relays during roundup. Two or three would eat at a time."

The work week on Kenedy Ranch lasted from Sunday evening to the next Saturday evening—with only twenty-four hours off. Gradually the hours were shortened. By the 1950s, the day started at sunup and ended around 5:00 or 6:00 in the evening, and at noon on Saturday. The hours on King Ranch were about the same.

This backbreaking work was done in primitive conditions. In the early days, vaqueros slept in the open out on the huge pastures, without any form of shelter until the 1920s. Then, sheets of canvas were sometimes used for some protection against rain and cold in winter. Eventually the Ranches issued heavy canvas tents. Jesús Gonzales of Kenedy Ranch said the men put "salt grass" (a grass that grows in coastal marshes in somewhat salty water) on the ground and covered it with saddle blankets in cold weather to try to keep warm. His saddle was his head rest. He shivered as he remembered ice forming on his hat and raincoat, then melting and running down his back. After the cattle drives ended and railroads came to Texas, the Ranch built cement block camp houses. They were located throughout the Ranch. Here the men could sleep, bathe, and have some of their meals cooked. Living conditions were much better then.

> I slept at camp on the ground in tents or in the camp house for twenty-five years. Wagons pulled by six-mule teams would bring the supplies and bedrolls. —Enemorio Serna (Kenedy Ranch)

There was no heat in winter, except for the campfire, and no relief from the searing heat of summer. Grit billowed around the men as they rode behind hundreds of cattle kicking up dirt clouds that seeped into every eye, ear, and neck, and any other inch of exposed flesh. If it rained, the grit turned to mud.

The men wore long pants and long sleeves, hats, and bandannas, even in the scalding summer, to avoid the dirt and the blistering sun. Keeping clean was impossible. Sometimes their clothes were so filthy that they had to wash them in the watering tanks, or in the creek, and sometimes they had to wear them wet. Wet clothes were especially miserable in cold weather. Most men tried to wait until they got home to get clean clothes, but sometimes this was just not possible. They missed their homes and their families.

Most of the men worked with cattle, but there were other backbreaking jobs. Nicolas Rodríguez of King Ranch was in charge of moving tents before camp houses were built. He repaired the tents and rolled them up, folded the bedrolls of bull skin, and readied all bedding for the move to the next location. The tents were very heavy, especially when they were wet, and it took all the strength Nicolas could muster to load them on mule wagons, at first, and later on trucks.

During the Great Depression in the 1930s, vaqueros were paid $.50 a day, or $15 a month, for this demanding work. By 1960, they were paid $90 a month, and by 1972, $120 a month. Housing and some food were also provided.

*   *   *

There were ghosts on the Wild Horse Desert. At least, many of the Kineños and Kenedeños thought so. Perhaps the ghosts were the result of vivid imaginations fanned by countless hours spent mostly alone on horseback on the vast acreage, but maybe not.

Seferino Gutiérrez claimed, "A ghost accompanied me to the next ranch many times, step for step."

Jesús Gonzales told of a man dressed in black appearing time after time while he was on his way to his father-in-law's house. And a lady in a white gown followed him until he finally lost her. Another time, he saw a lady in a white gown with hair to her waist, and he followed her to find out who she was, but she disappeared. He told of campfires in the distance on some mornings, but when he and the other vaqueros would ride to the place, nothing was there. He also said a man appeared and disappeared next to the water tower on Kenedy Ranch. On another ranch, he would see a fire three or four feet high, and when he would ride to it, there would be only ashes, with nothing apparently available to burn.

Ofelia Longoria of King Ranch, the lone woman cook of record, told of a headless horseman appearing in a pasture near where the Colony (housing units) is now located. Another story she related was of a man who found a bone in the Ojo de Agua Pasture and took it home. That night a lady dressed in white appeared to him and asked him to put her son back.

Many of the vaqueros' ghostly sightings happened out in the vast grasslands of the pastures where the shadows of a starlit night could produce unidentified images in the distance. However, some incidents occurred in an up-close and personal way. Enemorio Serna told a story that occurred in one of the camp houses on Kenedy Ranch. The vaqueros heard a man walking around with his spurs going click, click, click on the wooden floor. Then one night a cowboy was grabbed around the neck by a pair of hands. Needless to say, Enemorio and the others fled the camp house.

CHAPTER SIX

They Worked with the Best

His eleven-year-old grandson ran to the back porch and returned with Seferino Gutiérrez's favorite rope. He used any opportunity for the chance to see one more demonstration of his grandfather's amazing skill. He was not disappointed. First, Seferino described his own personal style:

> I used a Manila hemp rope and a turnover loop. I threw the rope overhanded instead of windup, and I was the head roper, the best, no competition. I roped between one hundred and two hundred cows a day.

Then, slowly rising to his feet, the eighty-four-year-old vaquero set about showing the proper way to hold the rope and demonstrated his famous skill, not by roping a bawling calf on the open range as in years past, but by lassoing a wooden chair there in his kitchen under the admiring eyes of his family.

Seferino was demonstrating the single most important tool of the vaquero, whose ability to use a rope would likely determine his success. All budding vaqueros began training with a rope at four or five years of age, and they practiced for hours every day. Manuel Silva, often called the most skillful roper on King Ranch, said, "I began by roping chickens, rabbits . . . anything that moved." His constant practice paid off. He explained, "By age fifteen I was an expert roper. I started working cattle. My team of three could brand a hundred cattle an hour."

Manuel Silva Sr. is known as one of the most skillful men with a rope on King Ranch. He was also in charge of handling the Thoroughbreds before his retirement.

Enemorio Serna was another expert roper on Kenedy Ranch. He said, "In 1953 . . . I roped a Mexican eagle and caught it in flight."

In the early days, lasso ropes were always made of Manila hemp fiber, and they were often greased with linseed oil or *sebo* (tallow) to keep them soft—for when they were wet, these ropes became almost as stiff as wire. Today, many ropes are made of nylon. Ropes used on the open range were forty to forty-five feet long, as the vaqueros could throw loops accurately at this distance. But shorter ropes of about twenty-five feet were necessary for use in the thick brush. Here the vaquero was lucky if he could get a chance to rope the animal's back legs by throwing the rope low, or he might lean over and throw the rope upward, which he hoped would result in his roping at least half the animal's head.

The vaquero might buy a rope to his liking, even though the Ranches furnished ropes. One thing was sure, the vaquero had to have a rope that fit him and his style because he depended on his rope and his horse to earn a living.

Some of the vaqueros even made their own ropes. Rope making could take on a religious meaning, as vaquero families often expressed their strong religious beliefs in their everyday lives. Albert V. "Lolo" Treviño, a famous vaquero of King Ranch, explained the symbolism of his hand-made quirt (short whip with a handle).

It [the symbolism] has been in my family for seven generations. You see, it begins with four braided strands representing Mary, Joseph, [my] Mother, and Daddy, then goes to three strands representing grandchildren in red, black, and brown, then finally braided down to two strands representing Jesus Christ. My daddy taught me what it meant and how to do it [plait]. My daddy taught me, "A cowboy without a rope is like a man without arms."

Alberto V. "Lolo" Treviño's family traces its roots back to the de la Garza family that lived on the Wild Horse Desert before Captain King came. A retired vaquero, Lolo is an expert plaiter and braider and works in the Visitor Management Department of King Ranch.

Lolo still makes *cabestro*, or hair rope, using an invention of his own to hold the hair while he braids the strands. He weaves the ropes from the manes and tails of horses. His designs are made from a wide variety of beautiful colors including silver, black, white, and all shades of brown and red. Lolo said, "These ropes are soft and unsuitable for lassoing, but may be used as a stake rope" (used for hitching a horse to a post). Lolo also makes fancy hatbands and bolo ties (plaited, rope-like necklaces).

Miguel Muñiz, at age ninety-three, also told of making ropes, bridles, and quirts. In his younger days, he was in charge of King Ranch Quarter Horses, and later became a master braider and plaiter after his father taught him these skills. He was so expert at making ropes that he could make two or three in a day from cotton wrapped in horsehair. They were six or seven feet long and five hundred pounds strong. Miguel's ropes were used to tether (stake) horses.

Miguel made his bullwhips and quirts from deer and cow skins. He knew how to tan (cure) the skins himself by rubbing salt and baking soda on them, then hanging them to dry. Miguel was also noted for his colorful plaited hatbands.

A vaquero depended on two things for a successful roundup: his own skill in using his rope and the quality of his horse.

＊　＊　＊

Captain King knew that if he was to have a successful ranch, he would have to have excellent horses. He also knew that his safety and that of his men depended on good horses, as bandits still roamed the Wild Horse Desert.

When Captain King started to upgrade his horses, he again looked south to Northern Mexico for help, just as when he had bought his first cows to upgrade his stock from Pedro and Anselmo Flores, who lived in Tamaulipas, Mexico. Víctor Alvarado wrote that his great-uncle, Damón Ortiz, sold and drove his horses to Captain King's new *rancho* on the Santa Gertrudis Creek. These fine horses were used to upgrade King's mustangs. Wild, low-grade horses had to be cleared out so the vaqueros could control the breeding program and produce better stock. Victor said that two bosses named Luis Robles and Julián Cantú worked hard to clear the pastures of these wild horses. They could not do it because there were just too many of them. The vaqueros were then told that they could have

Horses watering at one of the water tanks on King Ranch. *Photograph by Toni Frissell. Copyright © King Ranch, Inc., Kingsville, Texas.*

Horses coming over the sand dunes, Norias Division of King Ranch.
Photograph by Toni Frissell. Copyright © King Ranch, Inc., Kingsville, Texas.

the horses if they could catch them. The vaqueros soon cleared the pastures and often took the horses home with them. Julián Buentello recalled, "We killed out the wild horses and burros. If we caught them, we could have them or kill them. The wild horses caused a lot of trouble and scattered the other horses."

King Ranch continued to upgrade its horses after Captain King's death. It developed one of the foundation families that produced the American Quarter Horse. The Ranch bought a stallion called Old Sorrel. Old Sorrel was crossbred with Thoroughbreds, and the sorrel King Ranch Quarter Horse was perfected. In 1940, the American Quarter Horse Association was founded. In 1941, a grandson of Old Sorrel, Wimpy, was judged the grand champion at the Fort Worth Fat Stock Show and became number one in the Association's stud book. In 1984, the Association recorded its two-millionth registration. She was a filly owned by King Ranch, a direct descendant of Old Sorrel and Wimpy. Quarter Horses named Mr. San Peppy and his son Peppy San Badger (also called Little Peppy) became two of the most famous cutting horses in the world. At the end of 1999, Little Peppy was the all-time leading sire of competition cutting horses, his offspring having won in excess of $21 million.

While working cattle, all Kenedy and King Ranch vaqueros rode Quarter Horses, so named because of the breed's speed when running one-fourth, or a quarter, of a mile. The Quarter Horse was bred and perfected to do nimble cuts and turns to head off any calf trying to hightail it back to the brush or herd. The Quarter Horse is considered the best in the world for working cattle. The vaqueros were directly involved in every phase of its development and training.

The *remuda* was the group of fifteen to twenty-five horses used at roundup. Similar to "cliques" of cattle, the *remuda* had a leader, and this dominant horse often wore a bell around its neck. At dawn, the lead horse would bring the others to water at a circular concrete trough about thirty feet across that was filled by a nearby windmill. The vaqueros would stand in the center of the pen with their lariats (ropes) held by their sides, and the horses would begin circling the pen counterclockwise. The cowboys would each select one of their horses, as they had several in the *remuda* to use during the day as their mounts tired. The vaquero would then throw his lariat over the horse's head. The animal was trained to stop and wait for the vaquero. The horse was then taken to be saddled and was ready to go to work.

The *remudero* (worker in charge of horses) held a very responsible position because of the importance of horses to the work. *Remuderos* were nearly always vaqueros.

Each man rode several horses in a day—one to roundup, one to work cattle, another to ride back to the Ranch. Different horses were used to ride the brush. We kept the good horses out of the brush. We wore chaps and brush jackets. —Seferino Gutiérrez (Kenedy Ranch)

Martín Mendietta Jr. on King Ranch had an amazing ability to remember horses. If he was given the description of the mare and knew what stallion she was bred to, he could go into the pasture and find the colt. Martín could also look at a horse and tell what mare and stallion produced that horse. Every horse had a formal registration name and a nickname. Martín knew both. This was a valuable gift. Good records were very important, especially while the horses were being upgraded. No laptop computers were around to instantly record the description of the horses, but Martín always remembered.

The Mendietta name came to mean "expert horseman" in South Texas.

For five generations, Martín's family members were caporales (cow bosses). His father, Martín Sr., came from Cruillas, Mexico, in the 1880s and became a caporal on King Ranch. Javier Mendietta, his brother, was the next caporal. Then came his cousin, Valentín Quintanilla Jr.; then Sixto, another cousin; then Martín Jr. was a caporal for twenty-two years from 1963 to 1985. His cousin, Alfredo "Chito" Mendietta, is a caporal, or unit boss, today. As a unit boss, he has more responsibility than the caporal of former days. Each unit boss is responsible for a geographical area within the major land divisions of King Ranch. They care for the cattle and facilities, prepare a budget, and keep an accurate record of operations that are part of their geographical area. Their cattle inventory must include the age of every cow, how the cows are bred, and where they are located. The unit managers update their inventory daily and furnish numbers for the inventory report, which is published monthly. No other job is more important on the Ranch.

The Mendietta name came to mean "expert horseman."

Martín Mendietta Jr. is a fifth-generation vaquero on King Ranch. He and other of his family members were caporales (cow bosses).

Martín told how he and his father and brothers trained horses when he was little. They started by riding them bareback, then hooked them up and taught them to pull a buggy. Martín still remembers riding on the backs of buggy horses as a child. This helped the horses get used to having someone on their backs. Next the vaqueros broke or tamed the horses to the saddle so they could be ridden.

The Mendiettas had their own method for breaking horses. Martín Jr. told about the Mendietta method. They started working with the horses when the colts were a year old. First, they "halter-broke" them—managed to get a halter over their heads so they could be led. They rubbed and petted them, picked up their feet and rubbed their legs to tame them. After this, they branded the horses. The horses were marked with the Running W brand, the Ranch Division, the year, the sire, and the dam. The number was tattooed on the right leg. Mares were numbered on the right side of the neck with, usually, no more than three numbers.

Next, they took the colts away from their mothers and put them with old horses with bells on them—the males with an old male horse, and the females with an old mare. When the horses were two years old, they were brought back in and handled a couple of times. Their hooves were trimmed, and they were brushed and groomed, so that they would learn to be around the vaqueros. The Mendiettas did not finish breaking the horses until their third birthday. Martín Jr. described their method:

> We ran the horses in the corral for a few days, then mounted them. The old men would spread out in front and back, and we would trot, then lope the colts. The faster you got them to lope, the less chance of them bucking. We loped them from the corral to the bump gate— about a mile—and back. While they were winded, we stopped, started, got on and off. The next step was to work them a half-day. We did this every spring about April.

Julián Buentello was one of the best vaqueros at handling horses on King Ranch. He knew them all. Julián was boss of a *remuda*. Each man had twelve or fifteen horses, and if a man got on someone else's horse, Julián would remind him that he was on the wrong one. If a vaquero could not find his horse, in a few minutes Julián would whistle and would have spotted the horse the rider wanted. When visitors came to the Ranch, Julián was asked to choose the right horses for them because he knew the horses so well.

Julián was also a natural-born navigator. He never got lost. He always knew where the fences and gates were, even in the pitch-black night. Moving to the right pen or pasture was a challenge on the huge spreads of thousands of acres. Julián had the ability to always be on time at the right place with the lead steers. His father and grandfather had this gift, and so does his son, Raúl.

No matter how good the vaqueros were at it, breaking horses was a dangerous business. Wild horses dragged Jesse Salazar two different times. He was lucky both times because he escaped serious injury. Other vaqueros were not so lucky. Augustín Cavazos, who was working on the nearby Armstrong Ranch, was kicked to death by a horse he was trying to break.

The bump gate was invented to allow a truck or car to bump the gate open without the driver leaving the vehicle. *Photo by Betty Bailey Colley.*

This happened even though Augustín was not taking chances. He was breaking the horse inside a corral while his father and several other vaqueros sat on the fence watching.

*   *   *

One time in 1936, Robert Kleberg Jr. visited Kentucky and became fascinated with the Thoroughbred race horses he saw there. He began buying race horses and started a Thoroughbred program on King Ranch. In 1946, a King Ranch Thoroughbred, Assault, won the Triple Crown by winning the three most famous races in America: the Kentucky Derby, Belmont Stakes, and Preakness. He was one of only eleven horses ever to do so.

Assault was a miracle. Lolo Treviño was the vaquero who broke Assault. He told about the day Assault was born. Assault's mother was in bad shape, and the men were told to shoot both the mother and the colt. But, for some reason, Bob Kleberg decided to save the colt. Assault grew stronger and became a beautiful animal. When he was two years old and had just been broken to the saddle, he stepped on a metal surveyor's stake and split open his hoof. Again, Assault's future was in danger. Juan Silva, a vaquero, was a talented blacksmith. He rebuilt Assault's hoof and, after weeks of tender care, the hoof healed.

José García was Assault's exercise jockey. His wife, Nicolasa "Nico"

José García on Assault, the Triple Crown winner, in 1946, with Max Hirsch, Assault's trainer, beside him. José was the exercise boy for Assault and many other Thoroughbreds on King Ranch. *Courtesy King Ranch Archives, King Ranch, Inc., Kingsville, Texas.*

Quintanilla García, told the story of how José got this job. She said that José was sweeping the garage one day. A King Ranch boss, Lauro Cavazos, noticed that he was small for his age and asked him if he wanted to learn to ride the Thoroughbreds. José was scared. He had heard that these horses cost thousands of dollars and were sometimes nervous and hard to control. But he decided to try. He became a good rider, so good that he went to New York every summer to train King Ranch Thoroughbreds. The first time he went, he was fourteen years old. He kept going until after he was married and had four sons. Finally, he wanted to stay closer to home and work with the horses on the Ranch. Then, in 1963, one of the Thoroughbreds being trained in New York threw every rider that tried to get on him. Nobody could control the horse. Once more, José was asked to go to New York. He took Nico and his four boys and drove five days to get to New York. Again, José worked his magic, and the horse calmed down and let the jockeys ride him. Now, José and Nico's son trains and races at the Santa Anita race track in California.

Assault's Triple Crown established King Ranch as a major race horse breeder for twenty years. Just like the Quarter Horses, these horses were gently and expertly cared for, groomed, and trained by Kineños.

High quality saddles were necessary for Ranch work. Most of them were hand tooled on King Ranch and are still being made in Kingsville today. Martín Mendietta Jr., a fifth-generation vaquero, described the saddle trees (frames of saddles):

> Mr. Bob and Mr. Dick [Kleberg Jr.], owners, would have saddle trees made for us. We used Mr. Bob's tree. It came in fifteen or sixteen inches long, depending on your size, and you could order it like that. You picked size fifteen, sixteen, or seventeen, and the caporal [cow boss] would order for his men.

*   *   *

Captain King dreamed of building a first-class cattle herd when he established his cow camp in 1854. His dream came true. The history of cattle on King Ranch can be divided into four groups: the Longhorns, the milk-producing Jerseys, the Santa Gertrudis, and the King Ranch Santa Cruz. The world-class Jersey and Santa Gertrudis cattle were shown at major livestock shows, first in Texas, then across America and throughout the world. The Santa Gertrudis, developed on King Ranch, was the first American cattle breed. The King Ranch Santa Cruz was recently developed on the Ranch to meet a changing beef market.

*   *   *

Librado Maldonado lay in his bed one afternoon in 1980 with tears streaming down his face. He was eighty-two years old and paralyzed from his recent stroke. He was surrounded by a loving family, but his thoughts were somewhere else. Through the window he could hear the sounds of the King Ranch cattle auction. It was the first auction he had not attended. He was the "master showman" and was considered a legend in cattle circles for his ability to handle the prized cattle.

As he listened to the sounds of the auctioneer, his thoughts went back to how he began his journey as a master showman. He was born in 1898. He worked first with his grandfather at the Lasater Ranch. He remembered how his grandfather had been a tough boss. When, as a teenager, he would stay out late at night and sneak in, his grandfather would hear him, but would say nothing. He would just get him up at 4:00 A.M. and work him hard all the next day.

Librado remembered the day he was hired in 1925 to work with the

Librado Maldonado (on horse) with his grandfather, who brought him up on the Lasater Ranch. Librado was born in 1898, came to King Ranch in 1925, and became an outstanding showman of Jersey and Santa Gertrudis cattle.

Jersey cattle on King Ranch. He also remembered his cattle because he always treated them with the utmost respect and treated each one as an individual. He spoke to them in both Spanish and English and always thought of them as bilingual. Librado soon became the undisputed expert at training and grooming the milk-producing Jerseys.

King Ranch was in the process of developing what would become the first American breed of cattle, the Santa Gertrudis. Librado showed the first ones in 1928 under a tent in Houston. This first showing was only the beginning of Librado's journey with the Santa Gertrudis. People from all over the world would be amazed at how, with a soft-spoken "Hey, Babies" in an ear, he could command those two-thousand-pound bulls.

Librado moved these bulls to shows, at first by rail. He and his crew would load the valuable cattle in boxcars, making sure there was plenty of water and soft hay. The care of "his individuals" always came first. If the cattle needed more water, they got more water. He and his crew would just have to wait for lunch, maybe until two or three o'clock. When the cattle were loaded, Librado and the men would climb into the boxcars with the cattle. Sometimes the weather was hot, and sometimes it was cold. The dusty, noisy boxcars were not very comfortable, but he always felt better just being with the cattle and knowing they were calm. Librado took his own food supply, which was often canned sardines and salmon, beans, and crackers so he would not have to leave the cattle and go into a cafe to eat. When the train stopped, he and the men could get a cup of hot coffee to go with their cold food. He and the other men ate and slept only after the cattle were settled. If a show lasted until midnight, he loaded the cattle and started moving them to the next show so they would be there a day or two early. That way, they could get used to their new location before the show.

> ...with a soft-spoken "Hey, Babies" in an ear, he could command those two-thousand-pound bulls.

Librado must have smiled a little to himself as he remembered the airplane trip he and his son Beto took to Morocco, in northern Africa, in 1969.

King Ranch wanted to introduce the Santa Gertrudis breed to the African continent. Again, the owners turned to Librado for help. Planes were specially outfitted to carry the cattle. Librado and Beto and their crew loaded these highly prized two-thousand-pound bulls and flew with them to Casablanca for a two-week International Livestock Fair. Librado

Alberto "Beto" Maldonado with the 2,900-pound King Ranch Santa Gertrudis bull Macho. *Courtesy King Ranch Archives, King Ranch, Inc., Kingsville, Texas.*

was seventy-one years old at the time and had a lifetime of experience with these animals. He remembered how proud he felt to show them to the King of Morocco.

As Librado's thoughts drifted back to the auction noises, he must have thought about all the auctions he had worked in since 1950. That was the year King Ranch started inviting people from around the world to come to the Ranch to buy their famous cattle. People came from Africa, Australia, and South America. The Ranch gave big barbecues, and people would arrive in their private planes. Librado could still picture in his mind some of the famous guests who watched him show cattle in that ring. Winthrop Rockefeller and William du Pont of New York, Sid Richardson from Dallas and his nephew Perry Bass came. Even former Texas Governor John Connally was there, as was George H. W. Bush before he became the President of the United States. Librado remembered that even the King of

In 1985, Alberto "Beto" Maldonado took the 2,900-pound King Ranch Santa Gertrudis bull Macho to the Dallas airport to "buy" a ticket. Their appearance was publicity for their first airborne auction on the way to Hawaii.

Morocco once visited the Ranch after he and Beto had shown the famous Santa Gertrudis cattle to him in Morocco.

Even though Librado's days in the auction ring were ended, he felt proud that he had passed on his legacy of knowledge to his son, Beto Maldonado.

Plácido L. Maldonado (1921–1993) served in Africa and Italy during World War II and was awarded the Bronze Star for heroism. He later worked in the Veterinary Department on King Ranch.

Beto carried on his father's tradition and became the top showman of his generation. Like his father, Beto was known for his gentle way with, and respect for, the animals. He went to work with the Santa Gertrudis cattle in the 1950s, and kept records on them and showed them for more than twenty-six years. Beto said the Santa Gertrudis were so much bigger than the Jerseys he had worked with first that he had to add rails to the trucks to keep the cattle from jumping out.

One time Beto was asked to take the Ranch's prize bull, Macho, to the Dallas airport and buy him a ticket as a publicity stunt. Beto drove Macho to a friend's ranch on the way and spent the night. Then they went on to the Dallas airport for the next night so Macho would be ready the next morning. Beto said:

> I learned from my father to take him off grain three days before and off water the day before. I went over the path ahead of time. There were media there from all over. I walked to the ticket counter, and there were about 250 people there. Macho shined like glass and behaved like a gentleman. He weighed 2,900 pounds and stood there an hour because everybody wanted their picture made with him.

Beto's brother Plácido L. Maldonado left the Ranch to fight in World War II in the U.S. Army. He shipped out to Africa, saw combat in Italy, and was awarded the Bronze Star for bravery. Beto remained on the Ranch helping to produce beef, an important part of the war effort. Both sons remembered the strict routine their father, Librado, had developed for taming and grooming the Jerseys, then the Santa Gertrudis for show. They both followed his way:

TAME THEM

* Bring them into the barn and tie them to the stall fence. Check on them all during the night to be sure that they do not get tangled up.
* Untie them and lead them to water.
* One month later, put a halter on. ("He made the halter himself to get the right fit. He used a wooden piece to keep the halter from coming off.")
* Let them drag the halter rope and break themselves.
* Grab the halter rope, and tie them to the fence.
* Leave them there.
* Walk by to get them accustomed to people.
* Begin bringing them through a chute. Scratch their legs, backs, and heads with a curry comb while they are in the chute.
* Use a comb with a long handle so you don't get kicked.
* Turn out the bad ones.
* Lead them to a fence, and tie them there.

GROOM THEM

* Use a giant nut or bolt and screw it into the horns and attach leather straps so it can be pulled tight to shape the growth of the horns (Jersey cattle only).
* Brush them all over starting at the head and working back. Put blankets over them to make them sweat to shed old hair. Use a curry comb and get the old hair out.
* Condition their hair. Use a heavy rag and wipe from one end of the animal to the other. ("The rag would get lanolin on it from so much use on the natural hair. Everyone wanted to know what kind of oil we used. It was the natural oil of the cattle.")
* Clean the horns with a small rasp; smooth with emery cloth, shine with a little oil. (Beto said he wished for his Dad because "Today we use a sander and emery cloth and do in fifteen minutes what it took him an hour to do.")
* Clip ears, flanks, and switch-tails.
* Manicure hooves.
* Massage the udder and nipples of the females with oil.
* Teach them how to stand.
* Give them lots of tender loving care.

Dora Maldonado García and her daughter, Sonia Maldonado García, are knowledge-able about family life and growing up on King Ranch. *Photo by Betty Bailey Colley.*

Librado and Beto became the undisputed best at training, grooming, and showing prize cattle. They started a family tradition that continues to this generation. Librado's great-granddaughter, Sonia Maldonado García, was showing cattle by 1992. Sonia told about her first success:

My grandfather [Beto] was the one who taught me, "Don't take your eyes off the judge and never let go." The first Showmanship Award I won was in the seventh grade. I had tried so hard, and finally I won. I went blank for a minute, but I didn't take my eyes off the judge. There've been some times when I've been dragged, but I never let go. This year, I had the Grand Champion at the Kleberg-Kenedy County Fair.

CHAPTER SEVEN

Now Life Is Different

David Maldonado, a third-generation Kineño on King Ranch, has volunteered to show visitors a modern roundup. A graduate of Texas A&I University, now Texas A&M–Kingsville, he works as Director of Human Resources at the Ranch Headquarters. David brings his guests to the place where the cattle are to be gathered. He and the crew that will work the roundup wear Roper boots, not the traditional slanted-high-heel cowboy boots of the old days. David wears starched, creased jeans and a crisp white cowboy shirt with the Running W monogram stitched on the pocket. The crew's clothes are a mixture of the past and present. Leather chaps cover their jeans just like in the old days, but their shirts are plaid or tees worn outside. There are no cowboy-style shirts like those once so neatly tucked inside jeans. The men do not need their sturdy, canvas cloth jackets, the type that have withstood wear and tear on the Ranches for many years, for it is a beautiful, cool spring day.

Nearby, five horses wait patiently in big gooseneck trailers. Saddled and ready to go, they look like show horses. Actually, they are some of the sleek, cinnamon-colored Quarter Horses for which King Ranch is famous.

A vaquero scanning the sky with binoculars stands on the bed of a pickup truck. No cattle are in sight, only sky and bushy green mesquite trees. All of a sudden three dots appear on the horizon. At first, the helicopters look like specks, then like large mosquitoes. The helicopters come closer, circling the horizon. They sway and whirl as calves begin running from beneath the trees. The pilots know just how far to swing out to the right or to the left to get behind the cattle and move them to a clearing that leads to the pens. When some turn back, the pilots quickly move the helicopters to round them up—exactly the same technique used by the vaqueros working the cattle below. Two stray calves get away and head back toward the pickup. The vaqueros spring into action like a well-greased machine with moving parts. The calves have no chance. Each one is lassoed and loaded into the gooseneck trailer within moments. More than 90 percent of the cattle are rounded up with the helicopters. The rest are rounded up by vaqueros on horseback, the old-fashioned way. The job of gathering cattle from one pasture took fifteen cowboys a week to finish in the old days. Now it is completed in a few hours.

Like the Kineños on King Ranch, Kenedeños still work hard to make Kenedy Ranch successful. Like Kineños, they use both old and new methods. Enemorio Serna of Kenedy Ranch describes his work:

This vaquero on King Ranch stands on top of his truck looking for helicopters to appear for the present-day roundup. *Photo by Betty Bailey Colley.*

At first, I started with Longhorns, then Santa Gertrudis. Now I work with Beefmaster . . . The Beefmasters produce more and heavier beef, and bring more money . . .

We bring cattle in, separate them, put them in the chute, and ship from February to June. Today, roundups take from three to six hours . . . We use more pickups and fewer horses. I only ride [horses] now about twice a week. We use about fourteen men now; used to have thirty-five in a *corrida*.

*   *   *

Rounding up cattle with helicopters instead of from horseback is not the only change on the Ranches. Vaqueros' fathers and grandfathers slept under the stars on the hard ground. Now vaqueros can come home at night and sleep in their own beds. They ride pickup trucks now more than horses. Instead of eating their meals around the chuck wagon or at the camp house, the men may now eat at their favorite barbecue place, at a Mexican restaurant, or at McDonald's.

The way cattle are sold is also different now. When the famous cattle showman Librado Maldonado Sr. showed cattle at huge sales in the big auction barns, he never guessed that one day the prize cattle would be sold on television. Very often the cattle are videotaped and sold without the buyer ever seeing them. At other times, buyers just place an order for a certain number of calves weighing a certain amount, such as from 500 to 550 pounds. A price is agreed on, and the Ranch promises to have the calves ready by a certain date. The buyer sends big trucks to pick up the cattle. Auction rings stand empty.

Today sirens are used to gather cattle for feeding. Alfredo "Chito" Mendietta, a unit boss on King Ranch, chuckled as he told how well the cows are trained to sirens. Some boys were out of school for the Christmas holidays and were helping put out mineral blocks—big, yellow square hunks filled with minerals. One boy was standing on top of a stack of these mineral blocks. The blocks slipped and the boy fell, hit his head, and was knocked unconscious. Chito called an ambulance on his cell phone. The ambulance came into the pasture with its siren blaring. The cows heard it, of course, and thought it was feeding time. The medics loaded the boy in the ambulance and started out of the pasture. They were surprised to see three hundred cows in the road where there had been none just a few minutes before. The cows were bawling, looking for their supper. Chito had to get in front of the them and turn his truck's siren on so they would follow him. The ambulance could then leave the pasture and take the boy to the hospital.

The feeding of cattle is more technical and scientific today. They eat mostly grass and *mas carote,* cubes of cattle feed made on the Ranch. Feeders are placed by each watering tank, and when the cattle come to drink, they can snack on a few of the cubes. The mineral blocks are also nearby for them to lick.

*   *   *

Kineño and Kenedeño families value education today. Both men and women need new skills for work now, whether on or off the Ranches. In addition to learning riding and roping skills from their fathers to work the roundups, boys now must have a more formal education for different kinds of skills. Instead of learning from their mothers how to make soap, girls now are learning skills for the work place.

Ranch hands keep records of horses and cattle on computers. Fax machines are busy in Ranch offices where the workers have high school diplomas and college degrees. Technology makes all of the Ranch work faster and easier, but the work requires a different kind of training.

Public school education for Kineño children has changed a great deal since the first one-room school was built on King Ranch in the 1860s. Instead of the Big Chief tablets Beto Maldonado used, all students today in grades Pre-K through 8 at Santa Gertrudis School on King Ranch work on computers. Spanish is no longer forbidden as in the old days, but few youngsters want to speak it now, especially after they start school. David Maldonado said, "We used to get spankings for speaking Spanish in school—and now later, they hired my wife [Toni Maldonado] to teach Spanish!"

More students today finish the eighth grade and go on to high school. Now, students from the Santa Gertrudis ISD on King Ranch go to a much different type of high school designed especially for them called the Academy High School. The Santa Gertrudis Independent School District, the Driscoll Independent School District, and Texas A&M–Kingsville joined together to create Academy High School. It is located on the campus of Texas A&M University in Kingsville, and admits few students other than those from King Ranch and Driscoll ISD.

All students have their own education plans and follow a self-paced,

Students at Academy High School can build, network, and repair almost any computer by the time they graduate.

Courtesy of Academy High School, Santa Gertrudis Independent School District.

computer-based curriculum. A student can finish a course at any time. Portfolios are very important. One feature of the school is a student-directed conference each nine weeks with students, their parents, and the homeroom teacher. Using their portfolios, students discuss their strengths and weaknesses with their parents and the teacher. (Student-led conferences using portfolios are held in grades Pre-K through 12 in Santa Gertrudis ISD.) Students at the Academy must show what they know and that they can use the skills that have been taught. When they can do this, they go on to the next level. Some students finish high school in four years, some take less time, and some take more. The school is reaching its goals. The dropout rate has fallen from more than 40 percent six years ago, when students attended area high schools, to zero today. Since the Academy began in 1994, 100 percent of students have passed the TAAS (Texas Assessment of Academic Skills) test and have graduated. Eighty percent of all graduates go on to attend college. All students of resident King Ranch employees are eligible for a $500 college scholarship each semester. These scholarships are funded through the Santa Gertrudis, Laureles, and Norias Scholarship Fund. Money for the scholarships comes from the Santa Gertrudis Elementary Parent-Teacher Association and fundraising activities by volunteers on the Norias Division of King Ranch.

The Academy's business program, Academy Entrepreneurship, earned for King Ranch family member Stephen J. "Tio" Kleberg a 1999 Hero for Children Award from the Texas Education Agency. He gave a lot of support to this program. The program teaches students how to build, install, network, market, and repair computers. They set up all the computers in their school, network them, and teach teachers how to use them. Students are certified in three business applications, and they can repair almost any computer by the time they graduate. Students also learn desktop publishing and lay out their school newspaper plus one for the community. The skills they learn help them to get a job, college credit, or both.

Children of Kenedy Ranch employees attend school in grades Pre-K through 6 in Sarita Independent School District in Sarita, Texas, located on Kenedy Ranch. The school has been rated Exemplary by the Texas Education Agency for three out of the past four years. Sarita students attend high school in either Riviera or Raymondville, and approximately 90 percent of them graduate, according to Sarita Superintendent/Principal Mary McKenna. All Kenedy County students who apply receive scholarships to attend the college of their choice. Money for these scholarships comes from the John G. and Marie Stella Kenedy Foundation, fundraisers by school staff and parents, and donations.

David Maldonado, a third-generation Kineño on his father's side and fourth-generation on his mother's side, worked while he earned a degree in business. He said, "Tio Kleberg gave me the opportunity to work for the Ranch while I attended college." David described his job at Ranch Headquarters: "I work in Human Resources. I manage the pension plan, make sure our retirees get their checks, and help with any problems they may have." He could not do this job without a college education.

David Maldonado, a graduate of Texas A&I, now Texas A&M–Kingsville, is the Human Resources Director for King Ranch. *Photo by Betty Bailey Colley.*

Norma Martínez comes from two of the oldest families on King Ranch—the Quintanillas and the Mendiettas. Five of her nine brothers and sisters have earned college degrees. Her master of science degree is in geology. She works as a senior environmental engineer at the Hoechst Celanese plant in Bishop, Texas.

Enemorio Serna of Kenedy Ranch said, "Young people want to get their education. They work on the Ranch in the summer and take semesters off to get the money to go to school."

House work has changed a great deal, too. Nearly every home has all the conveniences, such as electricity, indoor plumbing, air-conditioning, automatic washer and dryer, television, and microwave oven. Many of the women work outside the home, either on the Ranches or in town. They spend much less time on house work and look for short cuts. "My mother always set the ironing board up in the living room," remembered Dora Maldonado García. "It was an all-day thing. There was no air-conditioning. I was good at ironing and still am till this day. Now I just throw the clothes in the dryer—right quick."

One thing that has not changed is the closeness of families. Catalina Maldonado talked about hers:

> My grandfather Librado [Sr.] told us many stories about the Ranch and about [our] family, in the evening after supper. My Dad [Beto Maldonado] does that, too. He runs across pictures and letters, and he'll tell me the whole story about the picture. He can remember years and dates and stories. My grandfather was kind, very friendly, loving, outgoing—lots of friends. My father is just like him . . . the way you see my Dad—that's the way he is. I wish I could be like him and not get upset about things. He probably has raised his voice, but hardly ever. I talk with him almost every day, and every time he answers the phone, he's always in the best mood. He's got a real positive attitude about everything. I went with him one day on his tour [through King Ranch Visitor Management Department], and I was pretty impressed. My parents never drank. My dad never really even cussed.

One of the biggest changes in the lives of Kenedeño and Kineño families is the amount of time they have to play. In the past, entertainment was limited to family gatherings for weddings, baptisms, and Christmas

In the 1950s, the King Ranch baseball team, "The King Ranch Cowboys," was one of the best semipro teams in Texas. Top row (from left): Alberto "Lolo" Treviño, Alberto Buentello, David Borrego Sr., Raúl Rodríguez, Alfredo "Chito" Mendietta, and José Buentello. Middle row (from left): Tony Rodríguez, Julián Buen-tello Jr., Cipriano Escobedo, Jesús García Jr., Raúl Buentello, and René Borrego. Bottom row (from left): Renaldo "Naño" Borrego, Gilberto Rodríguez, Reynal "Mr. D" Villarreal, Refugio "Chino" Rodríguez, Stephen J. "Tio" Kleberg, Valentín Quintanilla Jr., and Fernando Rodríguez. *Copyright © King Ranch, Inc., Kingsville, Texas.*

holidays. Activities connected to work, like roping contests, rodeos, and storytelling around the fire, were the only other activities for the men. Visiting was the main recreation for the women. Very little time was left for even these activities because there was so much work to do. Now there is more time for fun.

Though there is evidence that baseball was played in Texas as early as 1861 (the year the Civil War started), professional baseball did not come to Texas until after World War II (1941–1945). The teams in South Texas were called semiprofessional teams, with the exception of San Antonio's membership in the professional Texas League. Semiprofessional (semi-pro) baseball was made of small-town baseball teams of the highest play-

ing skill and furnished many a Sunday afternoon of pleasure for both players and fans across Texas.

Baseball was played as early as 1907 on King Ranch. In the 1930s,
formal games were played between departments of the Ranch, such as
the Dairy Barn, Thoroughbred, and Slaughter House Departments. Thus,
a tradition of baseball competition already existed when some Kineños
asked Ranch owners about forming a semipro team, and they quickly
agreed. The Ranch provided the materials and equipment, and the Kineños
built Assault Park, named for the famous horse-racing Triple Crown Winner, Assault. The Ranch's most famous team was first called the Lions,
then the Seven-Ups, and finally the Cowboys. Fans traveled from all over
South Texas to watch the games at Assault Park. The park had bleachers
that held four hundred fans and shade trees that appealed to many more
for protection from the hot South Texas sun. Sunday afternoons took on
a party atmosphere with barbecue, refreshments, and visiting as family
members and fans gathered by noon for the game, which was usually

Members of the 1956 "Laureles Cowboys" baseball team, Ernesto Quintanilla (left),
Hector Treviño, Gabriel Treviño, and Manuel Treviño, are from two of the oldest
families on King Ranch. *Copyright© King Ranch, Inc., Kingsville, Texas.*

played at 3:00 P.M. Usually a thousand people watched the games, and for big games, two thousand fans would cheer on their team.

In the early days, the Cowboys were razzed because they were so young. Most of them were teenagers. Once they played in Banquete, Texas, and fans were upset because Banquete had hired seasoned players from Corpus Christi for the game. They called the Cowboys "little boys." After the Cowboys won the game, the fans were quiet and had to admit that the Cowboys were good.

Some of the King Ranch employees who helped create the Cowboys team in 1948 were members of families that had been on the Ranch for at least two generations. Names like Quintanilla, Treviño, de Luna, García, Cantú, Longoria, Silva, Montalvo, Mendietta, Buentello, Nájera, and Betancourt appeared on the player and coach team roster of all King Ranch employees. These family members were uniquely suited for this team sport because of the camaraderie they experienced in their work as Kineños. By 1956, when the Cowboys were one of the best semipro teams in Texas, talented players from outside were brought in and eventually made up half of the team.

King Ranch semiprofessional baseball was similar to teams all across Texas, but there were differences. The Cowboys were not allowed to argue with the umpire. They were the only team whose members did not worry about getting hurt, because the Ranch furnished insurance for them. A major difference was that eventually Mexican Americans, Anglo Americans, and African Americans played on the same team at a time when most other teams were still segregated by race. Johnny Pinchback, an African American, was a quick, base-stealing second baseman and relief pitcher. A second African American, Willie Moore, played shortstop. Moore lived in Kingsville and worked in Corpus Christi and had no car. He hitchhiked the forty-five-mile trip every day and still managed to practice with the team. Pinchback and Moore were keys to winning some of the Cowboys' most important games from 1954 through 1957 at a time in this country when segregation was still the rule. The team's last season was in 1961. That year, Stephen J. "Tio" Kleberg, great-great-grandson of Captain Richard King, the founder of King Ranch, was an outfielder for the team.

Fans could always expect excitement at Assault Park when the Cowboys played. Heckling, cheering, and booing were allowed and were continuous and bilingual. Alberto "Lolo" Treviño, eighteen years old in 1948, was a curve-ball pitcher and outfielder. One day when he was pitching, "Lolo" said:

> I struck out this player and he immediately charged the mound. Then he shook my hand because, he said, he had never struck out. Everyone thought he was going to fight.

Julián Buentello also played, and his son Alberto, a seventeen-year-old pitcher in 1948, had the most wins in team history.

By the 1960s television and air-conditioning had moved people in the South indoors. Baseball fans chose to watch a major league game on television rather than sitting in the hot sun with dirt flying in their eyes. Baseball became a sport for young boys, Little League teams flourished, and semipro baseball ended.

One of the biggest recreational events on King Ranch is the King Ranch Rodeo held every summer. Only King Ranch family members, King Ranch employees, and their families can enter. No outsiders are allowed. Everyone competes for "Best All Around Cowboy" and "Best All Around Cow Girl" belt buckles, the top prize. Every year, King Ranch also gives an Awards Banquet where employees are recognized for every five years of work. Awards are jewelry, a medallion, or some other gift that the employee chooses.

Some of the men on King Ranch play on softball teams, and both men and women enjoy hunting. In the early days, Kineños could only hunt small wild game. Today, some are members of the Kineño Hunting Club and can hunt a wide variety of wild game in season. Because all of them have cars, families can go see movies in town, attend their children's activities, or go wherever they want.

A new business on King Ranch is tourism. Guides, mostly Kineños, now show more than 50,000 visitors a year around the Santa Gertrudis Division. They ride buses with the *turistas* (tourists). Beto Maldonado is one of the guides. First, Beto tells about the Ranch today, about its 825,000 acres fenced with enough wire to reach from Kingsville to Boston, Massachusetts. He mentions 60,000 head of cattle still on the Ranch and the approximately three hundred water wells still there to bring them water. Beto tells about 39,000 acres of farmland that grows milo and cotton. The

In 1993, these King Ranch employees received awards from King Ranch Family member Stephen J. "Tio" Kleberg for their contributions to the South Texas ranching tradition. (From left) Valentín Quintanilla, Jamie Quintanilla, Julián Buentello, Manuel Silva, Tio Kleberg, Rogerio Silva, and John Armstrong.

feed mill turns the milo into feed for approximately 250,000 pounds of feed daily for the 15,000 cattle in the Feedlot being fattened for market.

Next the bus stops at the Santa Gertrudis Creek, the place where Captain King built his first cow camp. Beto points out the Texas Historical Marker. Then the bus moves on to pastures of King Ranch Quarter Horses. Visitors may see a fight. The colts run with older horses, and these horses teach the colts the ropes. Colts act a lot like teenage boys. They push and shove until they get into a fight. Then the older horse steps in and breaks it up before anybody gets hurt.

The *turistas* see beautiful, interesting sights on the tour. They may see deer, wild turkeys, feral (wild) hogs, javelinas, doves, and quail. Bright-colored wildflowers cover the pastures in the spring and turn to shades of brown

Alberto "Beto" Maldonado conducts tours for the King Ranch Visitor Center on the Santa Gertrudis Division.

Photo by Betty Bailey Colley.

David Maldonado, a member of the Hunting Club, and his daughters, Anise and Lillie, hunt on King Ranch in season. In the old days, Kineños were only allowed to hunt small animals, like armadillos and rabbits.

and gold in the fall. Many of the trees are mesquites. Some are not much taller than a man, though others grow up to 12 feet high. Their brown trunks hold up brilliant, lacy, green-leafed branches—even in the dry climate of the Wild Horse Desert.

Sometimes the visitor bus stops at the pens, where *turistas* get to watch vaqueros work cattle. The tour bus travels on through pastures where the famous Santa Gertrudis cattle are grazing. Beto tells his guests that this first American cattle breed has stocked over eleven million acres on five continents. Now a camp house—once the cowboy's home away from home—comes into view. Behind the camp house are the Feed Mill and Feedlot. Six hundred to seven hundred head of cattle are shipped to market from here each week.

The tour bus slows at the Quarter Horse Barn. A gray horse is always here with the sorrels. Beto explains that this gray horse is kept in memory of the time when the famous outlaw Jesse James is said to have left a gray horse for Captain King to thank him after spending the night at the Ranch. Beto says that the Quarter Horse operation is smaller today than in the past, but the high quality remains. There are approximately sixty mares and some valuable sires still around. Vaqueros still care for and train them. Near the Production Office are the graves of famous King Ranch horses, including Assault and Old Sorrel. Visitors sometimes leave the bus to read their grave markers.

Visitors to King Ranch sometimes stop to see the grave markers of Old Sorrel and Assault, two of the most famous King Ranch horses. *Photos by Betty Bailey Colley.*

The bus pulls away and heads towards the New Colony. More than a hundred houses come into view. They were built for the Kineños across from the Santa Gertrudis School in 1949. From the porches of these houses, the old-timers can sit and enjoy the same Santa Gertrudis Creek that drew Captain King to the location in the beginning. They can also watch the Ranch's new breed of cattle, the King Ranch Santa Cruz, graze on thick green grass. Beto explains why the Santa Cruz cattle are better suited to our changing American eating style than older breeds. Their meat is still delicious to eat, but it is not so fat.

The tour ends back at the King Ranch Visitor Center. Visitors have learned of the long, colorful history of King Ranch and of the Kineño families who made it so successful. Some of the visitors go a few miles to the Henrietta Memorial Center in Kingsville and learn even more about King Ranch and the Kineños.

Tourism will now also become a part of Kenedy Ranch, owned by the John G. and Marie Stella Kenedy Memorial Foundation, and the John G. Kenedy Jr. Charitable Trust. Plans are underway for a museum to be located on the Foundation's Ranch in Sarita. It will be designed as a place for all ages to learn about the history of Kenedy Ranch and South Texas.

Museum plans include a visitor center with an audiovisual film, a display of ranch tools and wagons, a windmill, a butterfly garden, and a gift shop. Some of the Ranch's original buildings will be renovated and used in the museum complex. Schools from across Texas will be invited to bring their students for "hands-on" experience of South Texas ranch life, both past and present.

Today, several of the Kenedeños, including the Gutiérrez and Gonzales families, own their own homes in Sarita. Sarita East left the dwellings and some money to their families at her death. Other Kenedeños live in housing provided by Mike East in Sarita near where the proposed museum will be located. No doubt they will be on hand to demonstrate their expertise in ranching skills.

There are many changes on the Ranches, and the relationships of owners and workers are changing also. Great respect for each other remains. Perhaps the history of this respect can best be told in words from a description of the funeral on March 25, 1925, of Henrietta King, Captain King's widow:

> An honor guard unlike any other on the face of earth led the slow procession. The Ranch's cowboys, nearly 200 of them, wearing their range clothes, riding their range horses, accompanied La Patrona, who had always been their partisan, upon her final journey.
>
> At her crowded gravesite, during the hymns, eulogies, and last prayers, grey haired bankers from Manhattan rubbed shoulders with leather faced choppers from the lonely *calles* of El Sauz.
>
> When the casket was lowered into the earth there was a stir at the edge of the crowd where the bare headed horsemen stood. They came reining forward in single file, unbidden and uncommanded save by their hearts, to canter with a centaur dash once around the open grave, their hats down at side salute to Henrietta King.

Manuela Mayorga also summed up this unusual relationship between the owners and Kineño families when she quoted Mrs. Henrietta King:

> Mrs. King said, "King Ranch started with Spanish people and the King Ranch will end with Spanish people."

*   *   *

The percentage of Mexican Americans in Texas continues to grow. With the sweeping changes in education, public service, and economic progress taking place in the Hispanic culture, the future of the Wild Horse Desert and all of Texas may very well lie in the hands of Mexican Americans. Surely the working families of the King and Kenedy Ranches will continue to serve as important role models for Texans in the twenty-first century.

People Interviewed or Mentioned

Acuña, Martín. Martín was a Kenedy vaquero in the 1880s who drowned while crossing a river on the trail to northern markets.

Adrián, Josefina Robles. Josefina's family is one of the oldest on King Ranch. She worked with her father taking care of cattle while she was growing up on a *ranchito* in the Big Caesar Pasture.

Alegría, José. José worked for the Kenedy and King Ranches. A famous cook, he shared his recipe for Cow's Head.

Allen, Clyde M., Jr. Clyde is the owner of Allen Furniture Store in Kingsville. Established in 1926 by Clyde's father, the store later included a funeral home that served both Mexicans and Anglos.

Alvarado, Francisco "Pancho." Francisco was born in 1800 and was one of the first workers on King Ranch. He and his son Ramón built the first *jacales* on the Ranch in 1854. Francisco was killed in 1863 during the Civil War while protecting Henrietta King from Union troops.

Alvarado, Ignacio. Ignacio was a caporal who worked for Robert Justus Kleberg on King Ranch.

Alvarado, José. José is a descendant of Francisco Alvarado, who died during the Union Army raid on King Ranch during the American Civil War.

Alvarado, Ramón. Ramón was one of the first cow bosses and helped build the first *jacales* on King Ranch. He made many successful trips herding cattle up the trails to northern markets.

Alvarado, Víctor Rodríguez. Víctor was Francisco Alvarado's grandson.

His recorded memories of the founding and early days of King Ranch are in the King Ranch archives.

Bass, Perry. The nephew and heir of Sid Richardson, a wealthy Texan from Dallas, Perry attended barbecues and auctions on King Ranch with his uncle.

Buentello, Antonia A. Quintanilla. Married to Julián Buentello, Antonia told stories of her father, Valentín Quintanilla, on trail drives in the 1880s.

Buentello, Julián. Now retired, Julián was a King Ranch *remuda* boss who was an outstanding navigator on the vast acreage of the Ranch. The son of Roman Buentello, Julián told stories of his father's experiences taking herds up the trail.

Burwell, Charlie. Charlie was a Texas Ranger who came to King Ranch in 1921 and became the foreman at the Laureles Division in 1930.

Burwell, Mary. The daughter of Charlie Burwell, Mary grew up on the Laureles Division of King Ranch. As a child, she was the playmate of María Luisa Montalvo Silva.

Bush, George H. W. George Bush came to King Ranch to attend an auction and barbecue. He was later elected President of the United States (1989–1993).

Cantú, Julián. Julián was a boss on King Ranch who worked with clearing the pastures of wild horses.

Cavazos, Antonia. Antonia was Manuela Gaytan Mayorga's mother. She brought up her family on King Ranch and often prepared food for Henrietta King and her guests.

Cavazos, Augustín. Augustín worked on the Armstrong Ranch and was kicked to death by a horse while trying to break him.

Cavazos, Lauro F., Sr. "Larry" was a young vaquero who defended the Norias Division of King Ranch during the Mexican bandit raids in 1915. In 1926, he became the first Mexican American foreman on King Ranch.

Cavazos, Virginia. Virginia was Manuela Mayorga's grandmother. She and her daughter Antonia, Manuela's mother, prepared special enchiladas for Henrietta King and her guests.

Connally, John. While Governor of Texas in 1976, John Connally was present when Librado Maldonado Sr. showed a prized Santa Gertrudis bull on the third floor of the Adolphus Hotel in Dallas.

Cuellar, Teresa Mayorga. The daughter of famous vaquero Macario

Mayorga who competed in rodeos in Texas and Mexico, Teresa grew up on Kenedy Ranch. Her father worked on both the Kenedy and King Ranches.

du Pont, William. A wealthy New Yorker, William du Pont flew to Texas to attend barbecues and auctions on King Ranch.

East, Mike. Mike is the nephew of Arthur L. East (Sarita Kenedy's husband) and the great-great-grandson of Captain King. He leases land from the John G. Kenedy Jr. Charitable Trust.

East, Sarita (Sarah Josephine) Kenedy. Married to Arthur East, Sarita was born in 1889 to John and Marie Turcotte Kenedy. She took over the management of Kenedy Ranch after her husband died.

Flores, Anselmo and Pedro. Captain King bought some of his first cows from Anselmo and Pedro Flores, who lived in Tamaulipas, Mexico.

García, Dora Maldonado. Dora is the daughter of Dora and Alberto "Beto" Maldonado Sr. She grew up on King Ranch and shared a lot of information about the Ranch. At one time she worked in the King Ranch Insurance Department in the administrative office on the Santa Gertrudis Division.

García, Felipe. At first a vaquero on King Ranch, Felipe later worked for many years as a cook on the Ranch.

García, José, Sr. José was the exercise jockey for the Triple Crown winner Assault and other Thoroughbreds raised on the Santa Gertrudis Division of King Ranch.

García, Nicolasa "Nico" Quintanilla. The wife of José García Sr., Nicolasa worked on King Ranch for Mary Lewis Kleberg; she shared customs of the people on the Ranch.

García, Sonia Maldonado. Sonia is a fourth-generation García family member and a sixth-generation Maldonado family member on King Ranch. She carried on the tradition of showmanship and love of cattle established by her great-grandfather, Librado Maldonado. She worked for the Ranch as a tour guide in the Visitor Management Department.

Gonzales, Jesús, Sr. Born in 1924, Jesús worked with wild horses and as a cook on Kenedy Ranch.

Guevara, Juan, Jr. Juan is a fourth-generation vaquero who grew up and worked on Kenedy Ranch.

Guevara, Juan, Sr. Born in 1937, Juan is a third-generation vaquero who worked all aspects of Kenedy Ranch. He is married to Stella Cuellar Guevara, and Juan Guevara Jr. is their son.

Guevara, Stella Cuellar. A fourth-generation member of the Mayorga and Cuellar families, Stella shared information about growing up on Kenedy Ranch.

Gutiérrez, Seferino. Seferino was born in 1906 and was an expert roper and horse trainer on Kenedy Ranch.

James, Jesse. Jesse James was a famous outlaw. Legend has it that a stranger came to King Ranch and was offered lodging by Captain Richard King. In return, the stranger left a gray horse for the captain and told the vaquero to tell him that Jesse James left him a horse. Gray horses, believed to be descendants of this horse, can be found today on King Ranch.

Jones, Allen. Allen was a Black trail boss who took herds up the Chisholm Trail during the great cattle drives in the late 1870s.

Kenedy, John Gregory, Sr. Born to Mifflin and Petra Vela Kenedy, John helped his father on cattle drives to Fort Dodge, Kansas. He married Marie Stella Turcotte and took over the management of La Parra Ranch and the Kenedy Pasture Company after his father's death.

Kenedy, Mifflin (Captain). Mifflin was born in 1818 in Pennsylvania and came to Texas in 1846. He was a partner and lifelong friend of Captain King. He sold his share of the Rancho Santa Gertrudis (future King Ranch) in 1868 and purchased Los Laureles Ranch. Later he purchased La Parra, a 400,000-acre ranch near King Ranch in South Texas. Today this land is known as the Kenedy Ranch.

King, Henrietta M. Chamberlain. Henrietta was born in 1832 in Missouri and came to Brownsville, Texas, in 1850 with her father, a Presbyterian minister and missionary. She was a teacher who married Captain King in 1854 and moved to the Santa Gertrudis cow camp. Together they developed the Rancho Santa Gertrudis, which would become King Ranch.

King, Richard (Captain). Born in New York City in 1824, Richard came to Texas as a young boy when he slipped aboard a ship as a stowaway. In 1853, he bought the first land for his Rancho Santa Gertrudis, which would later become King Ranch. At one time, King Ranch included 1,250,000 acres; today it has 825,000 acres.

King, Richard II. Richard was born in 1860 to Captain Richard King and Henrietta King.

King, Richard Lee (Don Ricardo). Richard was born in 1909 to Richard King III and Pierpont Heaney King.

Kleberg, Alice King. Alice was born to Captain Richard King and Henrietta M. Chamberlain King at Santa Gertrudis in 1862.

Kleberg, Caesar. Caesar was the nephew of Robert Justus Kleberg, who was married to Alice Gertrudis King and worked on King Ranch for forty-six years. Much of that time was spent on the Norias Division in game (wildlife) conservation and development of the King Ranch Quarter Horse.

Kleberg, Richard Mifflin "Dick," Sr. Born in 1887, Dick was the son of Robert Justus Kleberg Sr. and Alice Gertrudis King Kleberg. He supervised the Laureles Division. In 1931 he was elected to the U.S. Congress, where he served for thirteen years.

Kleberg, Robert Justus, Jr. Born in 1896 to Robert Justus Kleberg Sr. and Alice Gertrudis King Kleberg, he took over the management of King Ranch after his father. He is recognized for his leadership in the development of the King Ranch Quarter Horse, the Santa Gertrudis cattle breed, and the Thoroughbred racing program.

Kleberg, Robert Justus, Sr. He was born in 1853 and married Alice Gertrudis King in 1886. He studied law at the University of Virginia. After Captain King's death, Robert helped his mother-in-law, Henrietta King, run King Ranch.

Kleberg, Stephen J. "Tio." He is a direct descendant of Captain Richard King, the son of Richard Mifflin Kleberg Jr. and Mary Lewis Scott Kleberg. Until 1998, Tio was the vice-president of agri-business for King Ranch, Inc.

Lea, Tom. Tom Lea wrote *The King Ranch,* published by Little, Brown and Co. in Boston in 1957.

Longoria, Ofelia M. Ofelia is from one of the oldest families on King Ranch. She was the only woman to work as a camp cook on the Ranch.

Maldonado, Alberto "Beto." Beto is a retired Kineño who worked with the Santa Gertrudis cattle. He is now employed as a tour bus guide in the Visitor Management Department.

Maldonado, Antonia "Toni." A teacher at the Santa Gertrudis School, Toni is married to David Maldonado.

Maldonado, Catalina. Catalina is the granddaughter of Librado Maldonado Sr. and the daughter of Beto and Dora Maldonado. She grew up on King Ranch and works in the administrative office on the Santa Gertrudis Division.

Maldonado, David. A graduate of Texas A&I, David is the Director of

Human Resources for King Ranch. He is a third-generation family member on his father's side and fourth-generation on his mother's side. He trained with his grandfather, Librado Maldonado Sr., then worked with his father, Plácido L. Maldonado, in the Veterinary Department. He is married to Antonia Maldonado and they have two daughters.

Maldonado, Dora. Dora was born in 1930. She married Alberto "Beto" Maldonado Sr., and she shared information about raising their family on King Ranch.

Maldonado, Librado, Jr. "Lee." Lee was Librado Maldonado's son and Alberto "Beto" Maldonado and Plácido L. Maldonado's brother. When they were young boys, Lee placed second and Beto won a first-place ribbon for their calves, probably the first won by the Santa Gertrudis breed.

Maldonado, Librado, Sr. Librado was the most outstanding showman of King Ranch cattle, both Jersey and Santa Gertrudis breeds. He was born in 1898 on the Lasater Ranch and came to King Ranch in 1925.

Maldonado, Plácido L. His father was Librado Maldonado. Plácido worked with him in the Jersey operation and later worked in the Veterinarian Department on King Ranch.

Martínez, Norma. Norma is a senior environmental engineer with the Hoechst Celanese plant in Bishop, Texas. She is a descendant of two of the oldest families on King Ranch, the Quintanillas and the Mendiettas. She conducted oral interviews and found that the first Kineños came from Cruías (Cruillas) in Tamaulipas, Mexico.

Mayorga, George "Choche." Born in 1907, George worked with cattle on King Ranch. He often played his harmonica to keep the cattle quiet at night. His father was Macario Mayorga, a famous prize-winning vaquero in rodeo competition.

Mayorga, Macario. Macario was a famous, prize-winning vaquero who represented King Ranch in rodeo competitions across Texas and Mexico.

Mayorga, Manuela G. Manuela was born in 1911 and grew up on the Santa Gertrudis Division of King Ranch. Married to George "Choche" Mayorga, she shared information about the social customs of Ranch life.

Mayorga, Teresa. Teresa, daughter of the famous vaquero Macario Mayorga, grew up on the Norias Division of King Ranch in the 1920s.

McKenna, Mary. Mary McKenna is the superintendent/principal of Sarita Independent School District in Sarita, Texas.

Mendietta, Alfredo "Chito." He is a unit manager on King Ranch in charge of cattle on 120,000 acres. He is involved with the use of technology on the Ranch, including the use of helicopters to round up cattle.

Mendietta, Gavina. Gavina shared stories of the religious life on King Ranch. She is married to Martín Mendietta Sr. and is Martín Mendietta Jr.'s mother.

Mendietta, Javier. He was Martín Mendietta Sr.'s brother and followed him as caporal on King Ranch.

Mendietta, Martín, Jr. A fifth-generation vaquero on King Ranch, Martín was head of the cattle outfit on the Ranch for twenty years.

Mendietta, Martín, Sr. Martín came from Cruillas (Cruías), Mexico, in the 1880s and became a caporal on King Ranch.

Montalvo, Pedro. He was a vaquero on King Ranch who taught his daughter María and her friend Mary Burwell how to ride horses.

Morales, Guadalupe. Guadalupe was a *mayordomo* (boss of a foot unit) on Kenedy Ranch who was in charge of building fences in 1940.

Morales, José María. José was a *mayordomo* (boss of a foot unit) on Kenedy Ranch about 1880 and often carried the payroll for the Ranch.

Muñiz, Miguel. Miguel was born in 1896. He was in charge of the King Ranch Quarter Horses and, in his later years, a master braider of ropes, bridles, and quirts.

Ortiz, Damón. The brother of Víctor Alvarado's grandmother, Damón drove twenty-five mares and a stallion from Mexico to Captain King's new *rancho* on the Santa Gertrudis Creek.

Quintanilla, Elesa Pérez. She was the wife of Valentín Quintanilla Sr. and they lived on a *ranchito* called Ormegas on King Ranch. She and her children once rode out a hurricane that destroyed their home while her husband was out tying down the windmills.

Quintanilla, Valentín, Jr. Valentín, born in 1907, is a second-generation vaquero on King Ranch. He was a caporal in charge of the *corrida* at Santa Gertrudis Division of King Ranch.

Quintanilla, Venuseriano "Niñe." Venuseriano was Rogerio Silva's brother-in-law who helped to train him when Rogerio first went to work with the *corrida* on King Ranch.

Richardson, Sid. A wealthy Texan from Dallas, he attended the auctions and barbecues at Santa Gertrudis Division of King Ranch.

Robles, Luis, Sr. Luis was a horse boss on King Ranch who worked with clearing pastures of wild horses. He was Captain King's bodyguard.

Rockefeller, Winthrop. Winthrop Rockefeller was a wealthy New Yorker who attended auctions and barbecues on King Ranch. He was later elected governor of Arkansas.

Rodríguez, Manuel. Manuel was kidnapped and later escaped during the bandit raids on the Norias Division of King Ranch in 1915.

Rodríguez, Marcela. Marcela lived on the Norias Division of King Ranch with her widowed mother, Manuela Flores Rodríguez, and her brother, Nicolas Rodríguez.

Rodríguez, Nicolas, Sr. Nicolas's mother was killed in the Mexican bandit raids on King Ranch in 1915. He remembered Texas Rangers being there. He began his boy jobs at Caesar Kleberg's house at Norias Division, where Will Rogers was a frequent guest. Nicolas provided valuable information about vaquero families in the early 1900s.

Salazar, Jesse. Jesse was a vaquero on Kenedy Ranch in the 1950s; he told about being dragged by a horse.

Salinas, Antonio. Antonio was born in 1913 and came to work on Kenedy Ranch at age twelve. His job was driving trucks to deliver equipment and supplies. He was married to Marcela Salinas.

Serna, Enemorio, Sr. Enemorio, a vaquero on Kenedy Ranch, was nicknamed Tequito, "Little Tick," because he stuck to a horse like a tick and could not be thrown off. His experience ranged from taming wild horses to using helicopters and portable pens.

Serna, Olga. Olga was married to Enemorio Serna on Kenedy Ranch and raised her family on the Ranch in Sarita, Texas. She told about the role of women and the sense of community on the Ranch.

Silva, Juan. A blacksmith on King Ranch, Juan rebuilt Assault's foot, making it possible for Assault to become one of only eleven Triple Crown winners.

Silva, Manuel. Born in 1905, Manuel was called the most skillful roper on King Ranch. He also trained Thoroughbreds on the Santa Gertrudis Division.

Silva, María Luisa Montalvo. María grew up on the Laureles Division of King Ranch and told about life there, especially the women's role.

Silva, Rogerio. Born in 1919, Rogerio was a caporal on the Laureles Division of King Ranch. He worked as a vaquero for fifty-six years.

Treviño, Albert V. "Lolo." His ancestors owned the land before Captain King purchased it. He is retired and now works with tourists in the Visitor Management Department of King Ranch. He demonstrates his skill at cutting cattle and his ability as an expert plaiter (braider) of horsehair ropes.

Villa, Faustino. Faustino worked with Captain King on the steamboats on the Rio Grande. He later became one of the early vaqueros on King Ranch.

Villarreal, Holotino "La Chista." He cooked for the cow camps and in the kitchen in the Commissary on King Ranch for thirty years.

More about the Wild Horse Desert

SUGGESTED ACTIVITIES

1. Brands. Below are some of the brands that were used on the King and Kenedy Ranches through the years. Each of these brands represents something unique that could be identified with the owners and recognized as belonging to the Ranches.

Using these brands as examples, make up your own brand using either a type of animal, vegetation, or initials. Remember:

* The brand had to be made into a branding iron, so it could not be too fancy.
* The brand had to be one that could not be easily branded over and changed by cattle rustlers.
* The brand had to be registered at the County Courthouse to be official.

2. Either individually or in small groups, write two accounts of a cattle roundup, using information from the book. Write the first one as though you were rounding up the cattle the old way by horseback only. Be sure to include how many men, horses, and supplies you would need, as well as how long the roundup would take. Then write an account of a roundup today, explaining how it would be done with modern equipment and technology, and compare it to the old way.

BRANDS

Below you will find some of the brands that were used on the King and Kenedy ranches through the years. Each of these brands represents something distinctive that could be identified with the owners and recognized by everyone as belonging to them.

This brand was the initials of Captain Richard King's wife, Henrietta King, and it was registered in 1859.

This brand was the initials of Richard King. Notice that the initials had marks added to them to make them unique to Captain Richard King's brand. This brand was registered in 1859.

This brand represented the brand of Richard King and James Walworth when they were in business together. It was registered in 1859.

This brand was Captain Richard King's cattle and horse brand. It was registered in 1869. There are different stories of why it looked liked this. In English it was known as the Running W and in Spanish as the Viborita, the Little Snake.

Captain Mifflin Kenedy chose for his mark the Laurel Leaf to represent his Rancho Laureles.

Courtesy of Nancy Tiller

3. Using the glossary, write a story using as many of the Spanish words as you can.

4. Pretending that you live on the Ranches in the old days, make up your own ghost story.

5. Using the food staples mentioned in Chapters 3 and 4 that the vaqueros ate, make up a menu for a week for a family or for the *corrida* (cow camp) out on the range.

6. If you were to have a *quinceañera,* describe what you would want it to be like.

7. Pretend that you were Elesa Pérez Quintanilla and describe how you would have felt during the hurricane.

8. Pick your favorite job on the Ranch and describe how you would do it.

9. Write a story about a day at school and the problems you might have if you did not speak English.

10. Choose your favorite person in the book and write about why you like that person.

11. Using the map of the cattle trails on page 38 and information in the book, write about a day on a cattle drive.

12. Using the drawing of a chuck wagon on page 43 and the cattle trail map, pretend that you are the cook for one of Captain King's or Captain Kenedy's trail drives from their Ranches to Dodge City, Kansas. Plan on feeding forty men for three weeks. Remember you will feed them something before they go out in the pre-dawn hours, then breakfast, lunch, and dinner. Write a description of what you would need to pack in the chuck wagon to go up the trail. Describe where you would pack all the things in the chuck wagon.

RANGE AND CAMP HOUSE RECIPES

★ Beans (*Frijoles*)

NOTE: *These proportions are for many hardworking, hungry men. Half of this recipe would be enough for a classroom or two. The beans can be cooked in crock pots by putting the beans covered with water in the crock pots before school is out to soak overnight, then adding the remaining ingredients and turning the pots on early the next morning. The beans will be ready in the afternoon. (The use or amount of jalapeños may need to be adjusted to suit the class.)*

8 pounds pinto beans	2 teaspoons comino
cilantro (handful, optional)	2 pounds salt pork (or bacon)
2 onions, chopped	4 fresh tomatoes, cut in half
2 red hot peppers, seeded and chopped	
10 jalapeño peppers, seeded and chopped (optional)	

Soak beans overnight. Place beans and pork in 10 gallons water. Add 2 tablespoons salt (or to taste). Boil 1 $^1/_2$ hours with lid on. Add other ingredients. Cook another 30 minutes. Serve with camp bread or tortillas.

★ Camp Bread
(Converted to indoor oven method)

5 pounds flour
5 teaspoons baking powder
5 teaspoons salt
3 teaspoons sugar

1 pound Crisco (vegetable shortening)
1 cup milk
5 cups warm water

Heat oven to 500 degrees. Mix flour, baking powder, salt, and sugar together. Mix in shortening, cutting it in with two knives or a pastry cutter. Mix milk and water together and, with a fork, slowly add to flour mixture, forming a soft dough. Grease bottom and sides of cast iron skillet or "camp bread" pot (black cast iron with three legs, flat bottom, and flat top for holding coals, available at some hardware stores). Shape enough dough to just cover the bottom of the pan; dough should be about $1/2$ inch thick. Bake 5 or 6 minutes. Re-grease before cooking next round of bread. Serve with *frijoles* or barbecue. (Ask if food service people can bake this after the students have mixed the dough.)

★ Flour Tortillas

NOTE: *Flour tortilla mix can be found in most supermarkets. Each student can make a tortilla using any clean, smooth-sided bottle as a "rolling pin."*

For 24 tortillas:
4 cups flour tortilla mix   1 cup warm water

Measure warm water in a bowl. Add flour tortilla mix and mix with fork until dough forms a ball. If dough is dry, add 1 teaspoon water.

Knead dough for 5 or 6 minutes. Cover with plastic wrap to prevent drying of dough. Let dough stand for 20 minutes.

Shape dough into 1- to $1 1/2$-inch balls.

Preheat ungreased griddle, comal, or electric skillet until very hot (450 degrees).

Roll out each dough ball to form a circle approximately 6 inches in diameter.

Cook 30 to 35 seconds on each side. Turn over again and cook 15 to 20 seconds. Stack tortillas together. Cover to keep warm.

★ Spanish Rice

1 ¹/₂ pounds regular rice	1 teaspoon garlic powder
2 tablespoons cooking oil	1 onion, chopped
1 15-ounce can tomato sauce	1 bell pepper, chopped
1 tablespoon salt	2 or 3 pieces celery, chopped
1 teaspoon ground comino	1 quart hot water

Brown rice in oil. Add other ingredients and cook with lid on about 20 minutes, or until done. Adjust seasonings. Feeds 20 people.

★ Buñuelos
(From the King Ranch Cook Book, *courtesy of King Ranch, Inc.)*

1 cup anise tea	¹/₄ cup shortening
4 cups flour	1 egg, beaten
¹/₄ teaspoon salt	4 teaspoons ground stick cinnamon
1 ¹/₂ tablespoons sugar	4 tablespoons sugar

Prepare one cup tea by boiling 3 teaspoons anise. Sift dry ingredients and add shortening and blend. Add beaten egg and lukewarm tea to dry ingredients and knead dough. Make small dough balls and shape into patties. Let stand for one hour. Roll out as thin as possible. Fry in deep fat until golden brown (prick tortillas with a fork when dropped into hot fat to make them puff). In brown bag, mix 4 teaspoons ground stick cinnamon to 4 tablespoons sugar. Toss fried crisp tortillas in paper bag to coat with cinnamon-sugar mixture.

Ofelia Domínguez, Lauro's Hill

★ Elva's *Carne Guisada* (Beef Stew)
(From the King Ranch Cook Book, *courtesy of King Ranch, Inc.)*

2 chuck roasts (for 12 people), trimmed & cubed

¹/₂ cup oil	¹/₂ cup flour
¹/₂ teaspoon comino	¹/₂ teaspoon black pepper
1 clove garlic	1 8-ounce can Rotel Tomatoes
1 onion	1 bell pepper, chopped

Trim all fat from meat; make sure that it is cut in small bite size cubes. Heat oil, put in meat and cook down to absorb all liquid, but not dry. Sprinkle ¹/₂ cup of flour over meat, brown well, add spices, stir, add tomato sauce, chopped onion and bell pepper, and 1 cup of water. Stir, boil 5 minutes, cook covered, simmer 15 minutes and serve.

It takes Elva thirty minutes start to finish.

Chon Silva, Laureles Ranch, Ojo de Agua

NOTE: *By the 1960s, tea and Kool-Aid became popular to serve with meals, and students will no doubt find these more appealing than coffee, which was nearly always available at mealtime.*

Selected Websites

Cattle Drives
      http://www.hppublish.com/oldwest/cattle.html

Institute of Texas Cultures
      http://www.texancultures.utsa.edu

Kenedy Foundation Ranch—In Pursuit of the Ultimate Bird Tour
      http://www.kenedy-ranch.org

King Ranch, Inc.
      http://www.king-ranch.com

King Ranch Cattle
      http://www.king-ranch.com/cattle.htm

King Ranch Guided Historical Tour
      http://www.king-ranch.com/visit.htm

King Ranch Museum and Henrietta Memorial Center
      http://www.king-ranch.com/museum.htm

The King Ranch Quarter Horses *by Robert M. Denhardt*
> http://www.premierpub.com/books/inprint/king.htm

King Ranch Saddle Shop
> http://www.krsaddleshop.com

Mid-Coast Santa Gertrudis Association
> http://www.santagertrudis.org

Our Spanish Heritage:
History and Genealogy of South Texas and Northeast Mexico
> http://www.geocities.com/Heartland/Ranch/5442

The South Texas Area
> http://www.taliesyn.com/ralph/stex.htm

Texas Historical Foundation
> http://www.texashf.org

Visit the King Ranch
> http://www.visit@king-ranch.com

GLOSSARY

amarosa—plant used by Kineño and Kenedeño families to ease stomach aches

American Quarter Horse—a breed developed in America and noted for its ability to run at a fast pace for up to a quarter of a mile. One of the four foundation families for the American Quarter Horse breed was developed at King Ranch.

Anglo—an Anglo-American, especially a white resident of the United States

armadillo—a burrowing mammal with a covering of armor-like jointed bony plates

bandanna—a cotton handkerchief, often red, used by cowboys to protect their faces and necks from the sun and grit

bandit—a robber

barbed wire—twisted strands of fence wire with sharp points located at regular spaces

bawling—crying out loudly

Beefmaster—one of the cattle breeds found on Kenedy Ranch today

boot—protective footgear, usually leather, covering the foot and part or all of the leg

Brahma—one of the cattle breeds King Ranch used to develop the first American cattle breed, the Santa Gertrudis

branding—using hot irons to burn a ranch's mark on an animal to show ownership bridle—a head harness for guiding a horse

bullwhip—a long, heavy whip used by cattle drivers

bump gate—a special gate that can be opened without leaving a vehicle by using the vehicle's bumper to tap the gate open

buñuelos—fried, puffed tortillas sprinkled with sugar and cinnamon

burro—small donkey

bush jacket—thick jacket worn by vaqueros to protect against rough vegetation in the brush country

cabestro—hair rope

cabrito—goat meat

calomel—a remedy used for easing stomach problems

camp bread. *See pan de campo*

caporal—the boss of a cow camp

carne asada—barbecue

carne guisada—beef stew

carreta—cart

chaps—heavy leather pants without a seat worn over trousers by cowboys to protect their legs

chorizo—spicy pork sausage

chuck wagon—a kitchen on wheels for storing, transporting, and serving food on the range and the trail

chute—a narrow wooden pen through which cattle are passed for tick treatment (dipping) or vaccination

comanche—an herb used to cure fever

commissary—a store on the ranch where food and equipment were sold

Confederate—a supporter or soldier of the South during the American Civil War (1861–1865)

conquistadores. *See* Spanish conquistadores

corrida—cow camp, the basic work unit of the ranches, in which ten to thirty men work together

cull—remove

culling—selecting and removing an animal from the herd

cutting horse—a horse trained to separate individual animals from a herd

dam—the female parent of any four-legged animal

despacio—slow, slowly

Don—a title of high rank and respect

El Sauz—a *rancho* once owned by Richard King

embalming—preventing the decay of a dead person by treating the body with preservatives

enchilada—a tortilla rolled and stuffed with a mixture containing meat or cheese, then baked

entrada—a procession of people or things moving forward

feral—a wild animal

foreman—a man who has charge of a group of workers

frijoles—Mexican beans, which were served daily on the Kenedy and King Ranches

GED—General Education Degree, earned by taking a test instead of completing a high school diploma

godparents—men or women who sponsor a child at baptism

hacienda—large rural ranch or estate

halter—a device made of rope or leather straps that fits around the head of an animal and can be used to lead or secure it

hearse—a vehicle for carrying a dead person to a church or cemetery

herd—a group of cattle or horses kept together for a specific purpose

homogenized milk—milk that is processed so that the cream does not separate from the rest of the milk on standing

jacal—a straw hut; wall construction was improved to include mesquite logs laid vertically with a mixture of clay, lime, and sacahuiste grass used to fill spaces between the logs

javelina—a collared peccary (a wild animal similar to a pig), common in South Texas

Jersey—a breed of dairy cattle once found on King Ranch

Kenedeños—Kenedy's Men, or the people who worked on Kenedy Ranch

kerosene—a thin oil made from petroleum, sometimes used for treating snake bites

Kineños—King's Men, or people who worked on King Ranch

King Ranch Quarter Horse—one of the four foundation families for the American Quarter Horse

King Ranch Santa Cruz—breed of cattle recently developed on King Ranch

La Chista—"little bird"

lariat—rope

Las Pastorelas—a traditional Mexican Christmas play often performed by Kineño and Kenedeño families at church

La Patrona—name used for Henrietta King by the Kineños, meaning patron, defender, protector, employer, or boss

lasso—long rope with a sliding noose at one end, used to catch cattle and
    wild horses

levántate—get up

Longhorn. *See* Texas Longhorn

lope—to move (a horse) along easily

lye—the liquid obtained by filtering water through, or leaching, wood
    ashes; used in making soap

Manila hemp—the fiber of a tropical plant used for making ropes

mas carote—cubes of cattle feed made on King Ranch

mayordomo—boss of a "foot section" charged with jobs other than cattle
    work

Mexican—a native or inhabitant of Mexico, or pertaining to Mexico's in-
    habitants, their language, or their culture

muy bien—very well

noose—a loop formed by a running knot in a rope

pan de campo—disks of flour bread cooked every day in the cow camps on
    the Kenedy and King Ranches

partera—midwife; a person who helps with childbirth but is not a nurse or
    doctor

partidas—holding pens where cattle were selected to go up the trail to rail-
    roads and Midwestern cities

Pastorelas. *See* Las Pastorelas

Patrona. *See* La Patrona

payroll—the total sum of money to be paid to employees at a given time

peso—the basic unit of money in Mexico and some South American coun-
    tries

postadores—intermediary, or go-between, for two families whose son and
    daughter want to marry

Quarter Horse. *See* American Quarter Horse

quinceañera—a Mexican celebration of the approaching womanhood of a
    girl, held on her fifteenth birthday

quinine—a remedy used to treat fever

quirt—a short whip with a handle

ranchitos—homesteads located in remote areas of a large ranch

rancho—ranch

rawhide—the untanned hide of cattle or other animals, sometimes used to
    make ropes or whips

remuda—a group of fifteen to twenty-five horses used for working cattle

remudero—person in charge of the horses

rodeo—a cattle roundup, or a public entertainment including competitions such as bull riding, barrel racing, or roping competition

roundup—the gathering of cattle for branding, inoculating, and separating for breeding or selling to market

saddle—a leather seat for a rider, held on an animal's back by a girth, or band, around the animal's belly

saddle tree—the frame of a saddle, usually made of wood

Santa Cruz. *See* King Ranch Santa Cruz

Santa Gertrudis—first American breed of cattle, developed at King Ranch

sebo—tallow or fat

siesta—nap

sire—the male parent of an animal

sorrel—light reddish brown color of the King Ranch Quarter Horse

Spanish conquistadores—explorers who traveled to the New World, including Mexico, to claim the land for Spain

stagecoach—a four-wheeled horse-drawn vehicle used to carry passengers, parcels, and mail

tallow—animal fat

tamales—native Mexican dish made of minced meat and red pepper seasoning rolled in corn shucks and steamed

tan—to cure, or soften, leather

tarpaulin—waterproof canvas used to cover and protect people and items from moisture

tether—to stake or fasten an animal to a fence or tree with a rope

Texas Longhorn—a breed of cattle with horns an average of four feet long, found on the Wild Horse Desert when Captain King arrived in 1854

Texas Rangers—law enforcement unit of the State of Texas

thoroughbred—pure bred, pedigreed

Thoroughbred—a breed of horses bred for racing

tortillas—small, flat, unleavened rounds of bread; staple of the Mexican diet

trot—a gait between a walk and a run of a four-footed animal

tuberculosis—a contagious disease of people and animals, caused by a micro-organism

turistas—tourists

vaqueros—Mexican cowboys who are descendants of the Spanish settlers and Mestizos, those with a blend of Spanish and Indian blood

veterinarian—a person trained and authorized to medically treat animals

Wild Horse Desert—the South Texas land stretching from the Nueces River south to the Rio Grande

windmill—a mill or other machine that runs on the energy generated by a wheel of adjustable blades or slats rotated by the wind; used to bring water to the surface on the Ranches

Yankee—a native or inhabitant of the Northern states, especially a Union soldier during the American Civil War (1861–1865)

BIBLIOGRAPHY

BOOKS

Adams, Ramon F. *Come an' Get It.* Norman: University of Oklahoma Press, 1952.

Atherton, Lewis. *The Cattle Kings,* pp. 263–278. Bloomington: Indiana University Press, 1961.

Brown, Dee. *Cowboys: Trail Driving Days.* New York: Scribner's, 1952.

Brown, Mark. *Cowboys: Before Barbed Wire.* New York: Holt, 1956.

Cypher, John. *Bob Kleberg and the King Ranch: A Worldwide Sea of Grass.* Austin: University of Texas Press, 1995.

Dary, David. *Cowboy Culture.* Lawrence: University Press of Kansas, 1989.

Denhardt, Robert M. *The King Ranch Quarter Horses.* Norman: University of Oklahoma Press, 1970.

Dobie, J. Frank. *Cow People.* Boston: Little, Brown, 1964; reprint, Austin: University of Texas Press, 1981.

———. *A Vaquero of the Brush Country: Partly from the Reminiscences of John Young.* New York: Grosset and Dunlap, 1929; Austin: University of Texas Press, 1981. Reprinted as John D. Young and J. Frank Dobie, *A Vaquero of the Brush Country: The Life and Times of John D. Young.* Austin: University of Texas Press, 1998.

Frissell, Toni. *The King Ranch, 1939–1944.* New York: Morgan & Morgan, 1975.

Frost, Dick. *The King Ranch Papers.* Chicago: Aquarius Rising Press, 1985.

————. *La Madonna Goes to the Big Rancho in the Sky.* Chicago: Aquarius Rising Press, 1985.

Goodwyn, Frank. *Life on the King Ranch.* New York: Crowell, 1951.

Graham, Joe S. *El Rancho in South Texas.* Denton: University of North Texas Press, 1994.

Harper, Minnie Timms, and George Dewey Harper. *Old Ranches.* Dallas: Dealey and Lowe, 1936.

King, Edward, and T. Wells Champney. *Texas 1874.* Lincoln, Mass.: Cordovan Press, 1974.

King Ranch: 100 Years of Ranching. Corpus Christi, Tex.: *Corpus Christi Caller-Times,* 1953.

King Ranch Cookbook. Kingsville: King Ranch, 1992.

Lea, Tom. *The King Ranch.* 2 vols. Boston: Little, Brown and Company, 1957.

Lomax, John. *Cow Camps and Cattle Herds.* Austin: Encino Press, 1967.

Michaud, Stephen G., and Hugh Aynesworth. *If You Love Me You Will Do My Will.* New York: W. W. Norton & Company, 1990.

Monday, Jane Clements, and Betty Bailey Colley. *Voices from the Wild Horse Desert: The Vaquero Families of the King and Kenedy Ranches.* Austin: University of Texas Press, 1997.

Montejano, David. *Anglos and Mexicans in the Making of Texas, 1836–1986.* Austin: University of Texas Press, 1987, 1992.

Munson, Sammye. *Our Tejano Heroes.* Austin: Panda Books, 1989.

Myers, Sandra L. *The Ranch in Spanish Texas, 1691–1800.* El Paso: Texas Western Press, 1969.

Nordyke, Lewis. *Cattle Empire: The Fabulous Story of the 3,000,000 Acre XIT.* New York: William Morrow, 1949.

O'Conner, Louise. *Crying for Daylight: A Ranching Culture in the Texas Coastal Bend.* Austin: Wexford Publishing, 1989.

Robertson, Brian. *Wild Horse Desert: The Heritage of South Texas.* Edinburg, Tex.: Santander Press, 1985.

Steiner, Stan. *The Ranchers.* Norman: University of Oklahoma Press by arrangement with Alfred A. Knopf, 1985.

Thompson, Jerry. *A Wild and Vivid Land.* Austin: Texas State Historical Association, 1997.

Ward, Delbert R. *Great Ranches of the United States,* pp. 78–82. San Antonio: Ganado Press, 1993.

Ward, Fay E. *The Working Cowboy's Manual.* New York: Bonanza Books, 1983.

Welch, June Rayfield. *The Glory That Was Texas.* Waco: Texian Press, 1975.

Witliff, William O. *Vaquero-Genesis of the Texas Cowboy.* San Antonio: University of Texas Institute of Texas Cultures, 1972.

BULLETINS

Alvarado, Víctor Rodríguez. *Memoirs.* Translation. Kingsville: King Ranch Archives, Henrietta Memorial Center, 1937.

Goodwyn, Frank. *Folk-Lore of the King Ranch Mexicans.* Reprint, Publications of the Texas Folk-Lore Society, vol. 9, 1931.

Kleberg, Robert J., Jr. *The Santa Gertrudis Breed of Beef Cattle.* Kingsville: King Ranch, May 1954.

The Mexican Texans. San Antonio: University of Texas Institute of Texan Cultures, 1986.

ARTICLES

Alexander, Sandy. "Retired Cowboy Feels He Was Destined for Job." *Kingsville Record*, date unknown.

"America's Cowboys: A History." *Cobblestone*, vol. 3, no. 7 (July 1982), pp. 4–48.

Barnhardt, Lee Ann. "Learning at the Center of New High School Concept." *Kingsville Record*, February 2, 1994, pp. 1, 3.

"Big as All Outdoors." *Time*, December 15, 1947, pp. 89–96.

Broyles, William, Jr. "The King Ranch." *Texas Monthly*, October 1980, pp. 150–173.

"Cattle Showman Librado Maldonado Known in Falfurrias." *Falfurrias Facts*, February 17, 1983.

Currie, Barton W. "A Farm As Big As Delaware." *The Country Gentleman* (Philadelphia), August 28, 1915, pp. 1, 4, 24.

Dobie, J. Frank. "The Magician on Horseback." *Mexican Life*, vol. 30, no. 5 (May 1955), pp. 11–14.

———. "The Mexican Vaquero of the Texas Border." Reprint, *Southwestern Political and Social Science Quarterly*, vol. 8, no. 1 (June 1927).

Erramouspe, Roxanne. "Today's King Ranch." *The Cattleman*, September 1995, pp. 10–32.

"King Ranch Today." *Western Horseman,* May 1980, pp. 37–45.

"King Ranch Tour One of Many Kingsville Attractions." *Traveling Historic Texas,* February/March 1991, pp. 1–8.

"King-Sized Changes." *National Cattlemen,* April 1987, pp. 13–14.

"Lauro Cavazos." *Dallas Morning News,* August 20, 1989, pp. 1–3E.

Lea, Tom. "The Mighty Ranch of Richard King." *Life,* July 8, 1957, pp. 37–44.

Markus, Kurt. "Five Generations of Horsemen." *Western Horseman,* April–May 1980, pp. 37–45.

Morrison, Dan. "The Right Gear." *Texas Highways,* September 1994, pp. 7–13.

Mullen, Joan. "A High School and University in One." *ATPE News,* September/October 1994.

Murphy, Charles J. V. "The Fabulous House of Kleberg: A World of Cattle and Grass." 3 parts. *Fortune,* June 1969, July 1969, August 1969.

Myers, Cindi. "Texas Giant." *Historic Traveler,* January 1996, pp. 26–37.

Nash, Susan Hawthorne. "Mystique in the Mesquite." *Southern Living,* February 1994, pp. 86–93.

Norvell, Scott. "Vaquero Tradition Immortalized in Exhibit." *Corpus Christi Caller Times,* September 18, 1989.

Quellhorst, Sherry. "Retired Ranch Employee Branding Iron Specialist." *Kingsville Record,* August 2, 1989.

Rhoad, A. O. "The Santa Gertrudis Breed." *Journal of Heredity,* vol. XL, no. 5 (May 1949), pp. 115–126.

Rhoad, A. O., and R. J. Kleberg Jr. "The Development of a Superior Family of the Modern Quarter Horse." *Journal of Heredity,* vol. XXXVII, no. 8 (August 1946), pp. 227–238.

Rosenblatt, George L. "Home on the Range." *Texas Highways,* September 1994, pp. 24–29.

Ruiz, Marco A. "Lonesome Legacies." *Dallas Morning News,* September 1, 1991.

Smallwood, Lanette. "Alberto 'Lolo' Treviño, King Ranch Celebrity." *Traveler,* March 1994, pp. 38–39.

Stanush, Barbara. "Only in Wild Horse Desert Would You Find King Ranch." *San Antonio Express-News,* July 25, 1992.

Tedford, Deborah. "Muñoz Named Candidate for Marshall." *Houston Chronicle,* April 15, 1995, Sec. A, p. 25.

Wolfshohl, Karl. "Birth of a New Breed." *Progressive Farmer*, February 1995, pp. 44–50.

"The World's Biggest Ranch." *Fortune*, December 1933, pp. 48–109.

UNPUBLISHED SOURCES

Cheeseman, Bruce S. "History of Santa Gertrudis School." Unpublished manuscript, King Ranch Archives, Kingsville.

Kenedy Ranch Ledger Books. Corpus Christi Museum of Science and History.

King Ranch Ledger Books. King Ranch Archives, Henrietta Memorial Center, Kingsville.

Lopez, Donavan. "Practice! Practice! Practice! The History of the King Ranch Cowboys Baseball Team." Master's thesis, Texas A&M University–Kingsville, 1999.

Neely, Lisa A. "Folklore of Los Kineños." Graduate paper in Gothic Literature, Texas A&I University, November 30, 1993.

Villarreal, Roberto M. "The Mexican-American Vaqueros of Kenedy Ranch: A Social History." Master's thesis, Texas A&I University, 1972.

Young, Andrew Herbert. "Life and Labor on the King Ranch: 1853–1900." Master's thesis, Texas A&I University, 1992.

INDEX